MW00963851

ART IS DEAD

David L. Gersh

Printed in the United States of America.

For information address:
Durban House Publishing Company, Inc.
7502 Greenville Avenue, Suite 500, Dallas, Texas 75231

Library of Congress Cataloging-in-Publication Data
Gersh, David L., 1942 -

Art Is Dead / David L. Gersh

Library of Congress Control Number: 2005937574

p. cm.

ISBN 1-930754-89-2
First Edition

10 9 8 7 6 5 4 3 2 1

Visit our Web site at
http://www.durbanhouse.com

PUPPIES IS GRAND AND GLORIOUS CREATURES.

THIS BOOK IS FOR YOU.

Acknowledgments

Writing a book, particularly a first book, is a precarious process. You're constantly teetering on the edge. If you're like me, you let a lot of people read it, getting a lot of feedback, hoping someone will love it and tell you it's perfect. That doesn't happen, of course.

I was talking to my son, Steven, about the process of trying to write a book. He made an interesting observation. He asked me, "What would Picasso have said if someone had pointed to one of his paintings and said, 'That should be yellow.'?"

I always thought writing was a solitary and internal process. In fact, if it didn't take a village, at least it took a very extended family. So let me try to set about giving my thanks to some of the people who helped.

First and foremost, to my wife and best buddy, Stella Zadeh, I owe enormous gratitude for all the help she gave me in her comments from the endless reading of endless drafts, and for her astute and insightful advice in getting the book sold. Bob Middlemiss, my editor from Durban House, is a throwback to the great age of editors. As a friend said when he looked over one of Bob's letters to me outlining his comments, "Max Perkins, watch your laurels." And that was from a writer who is capable of distinguishing. Bob is thoughtful, encouraging and tough. Altogether, a great teacher. I really went to school on him, and to the extent that I could learn anything, I will be forever grateful.

My dear friend Harvey Champlin read every draft of every book that I've written and always gave me useful comments. He has helped me immeasurably. Fanny

Pereire was my muse. She is the delightful young French woman who talked to me about her work at Christie's and the art auction business and started me thinking about the subject of the art world, which has fascinated me for the last 15 years.

David Rintels was a source of constant encouragement. Boy, did I need it. Tish Nettleship read the 5th draft of this book and gave me detailed, page-by-page comments, several of which resulted in revisions and, I think, made a better book.

Many of my friends took their time to read my manuscript and make helpful comments. Their enthusiasm encouraged me. In alphabetical order, barring any more useful arrangement, I want to give my thanks to Meg Barbour, Noah benShea, Peter and Karen Brill, Jerry Cohen, Richard Cohen, Jane DeHart, Dawn Dyer, Mark and Missy Gersh, Allan Ghitterman, Micalyn Harris, Lauren Lucier, Kandy Luria, Clark Miller, Bob Temkin, Joe Tumbler and Tom Weinberger. Bless their hearts.

And thank you to Mike and Gaye Brockelbank at Piney Creek Kennel for providing us our great pug images. One final "thank you" to Sheldon McArthur, formerly of the Mystery Bookstore in Beverly Hills. Out of the goodness of his heart, he read my manuscript, and his comments pumped me up when things got tough.

Chapter one

"It was the dog that did it."

"Lady, are you telling me a dog killed the guy in there?"

"Don't be ridiculous, Lieutenant, of course not." She didn't like this thick-bodied, rumpled little man with the probing eyes. "It's what depressed poor Arthur so much and drove him back to drugs. At least, that's what I think. He loved that pug. Somebody stole it a month ago."

It was ten in the morning and Lt. Julian Wayne was standing in the living room of Arthur DeRuk's spacious East-side apartment, staring incredulously at the small, trim, well-turned-out woman in front of him. There was something unusual about her gray-green eyes that he couldn't figure out. She was framed against a Chinese red wall. He'd never seen a room done entirely in red before.

"Let me get this straight. This guy had a drug problem?"

She appeared to be in her mid 50s, but it was hard to

tell these days. Her eyes were young, even with the tiny webs of laugh lines at the corners. The 911 call had come in an hour earlier. The paramedics had called the police. The streets were icy from the freezing rain and it had taken some time to respond. Mimi Aaron was waiting in the front room when they arrived. She seemed composed, which struck Wayne as peculiar. He was having trouble concentrating.

It's hot in here, he thought, tugging at his collar. He shrugged off his raincoat but held it awkwardly over his arm. He didn't want to put it down until the Crime Scene people had time to go over the place. Where were they anyway? He tugged at his collar again. What had they been talking about? Oh yeah, the guy's drug problem. He looked up at the woman, waiting for a response.

"He used to," answered Mimi, "but he quit. He gave up alcohol and drugs. He had been in one of those programs for the last three months." She turned slightly and he caught a whiff of expensive perfume.

"How do you know so much about this guy?" He looked down at her hands. Hands always told him something. She was the exception. Hers were clasped delicately in front of her.

"Arthur and I were good friends."

"Exactly how good, Mrs. Aaron?"

"Lieutenant, I don't like your tone." She drew herself up. "Mr. DeRuk was a famous artist, and he and I had known each other a long time." The large diamond in her ring caught the light as she raised her hand to make her point. She had no intention of discussing her personal life with this pushy little man. Why did he keep tugging at his collar like that?

"What made you show up here today?"

She looked straight at him, her eyes calm. Watchful.

"I told you. Arthur had been depressed. I was concerned. So I came over to see if he was all right. To cheer him up."

"And you discovered the body."

"Yes. It was awful." Her hands sought each other again, gracefully.

She didn't make discovering the body seem so awful, Wayne reflected. Why was that?

"How'd you get in?"

"I have a key."

"I see."

"No, I suspect you don't, Lieutenant," she said in an arch tone. "But it's none of your business."

Wayne's face didn't register her rebuff. He'd had worse. But he didn't like it. "So exactly what happened after you let yourself in?"

"I called out to Arthur, but no one answered. I thought no one was home." She turned away and walked to the window. She wanted to get away from that rough-cut face. Those demanding brown eyes that seemed so cold. She turned back. A safer distance. "So I brought the soup into the kitchen to put it in the refrigerator."

"Soup?"

"Chicken soup. It was a standing joke between us."

"Oh?"

She took two steps towards him and pointed into the kitchen. She struggled to maintain control. "Then I sat down at the kitchen table to write Arthur a note."

"This the one?"

"Yes, that's it."

"Go on." He wanted to break that poised voice.

"As I was getting ready to leave, I noticed the bedroom door was closed. So I knocked. When no one answered, I opened the door. There was poor Arthur lying on his side across the bed with a syringe stuck in his arm." Her eyes widened at the memory. She fought back the emotion.

"And?"

"I rushed over and pulled the needle out, of course, and rolled him over on his back."

"So we'll find your fingerprints all over the syringe. Now tell me why you'd do a thing like that?" Was this woman nuts? Didn't she realize how all this looked? "You know you were destroying evidence?"

"This isn't the first time I've seen Arthur like this, Lieutenant," she said firmly, her manicured finger turning the diamond ring on her hand, making the stone flash again. "I thought he was sleeping it off. I didn't think he was dead."

"Sure. What'd you do then?"

"When I couldn't wake him up, I called 911 and waited."

"Okay. Anything else?"

"No."

"Leave your name and phone number with Inspector Tritter over there," he said, gesturing absently to a younger man across the room. "Address too, please. We may have some more questions later." You better believe it.

He watched her leave, gently closing the door. All form over content, these rich people. Think they're better than everyone. "So, what do you think?" he asked, crossing over to Tritter. "Besides that this apartment's too hot."

Tritter shrugged. He didn't feel warm.

"You read the papers, Tritter? You know who these people are?"

"No." The less said, the better, in Tritter's experience.

"Lady's Simon Aaron's ex-wife. Big socialite type. Rich. Guy's some looney-tunes artist, always doing something weird."

"So what do you think, Lieutenant?" Always a good response.

"I got an itch about this one," Wayne said, scratching at his neck with his stubby fingers. What was it about her eyes? Something was bothering him. He caught his rumpled reflection in the hall mirror, staring into his own cynical brown eyes.

Chapter two

The morning was silent, an ancient touch to the land. The cold had settled onto its fields. The stillness was broken only by an occasional crack in the small copse of birches and elms when a tree shed its nighttime coat of ice as the sun warmed it. Sparkling crystals fell into the returning stillness.

Jonathan Benjamin Franklin loved living on his seven good acres of land in Concord, in his old two-story clapboard house. And he especially loved having Nicole here with him today. He looked down at her through his wire-rimmed glasses as they walked hand in hand, bundled up against the cold. The scarlet cashmere scarf she had pulled over her ears framed her dark hair above gray, lively eyes. Not exactly beautiful, her classic features still gave her face a sense of something complete and elegant.

"I love your sense of style," he said.

Her tinkling laugh sounded like the crystal shower of ice falling to the snow. It had been four years and their relationship had deepened. That alone was a wonder to him. He wouldn't have believed it a few years ago.

He was fairly rich, but she had ten times more money than he did. Besides, she earned a lot more since he had given up his law practice to teach at Harvard. It's a good thing I'm not too insecure, he reflected, looking up into the snow-shrouded trees. That brought a smile to his face.

"Are you happy, *cheri*?" Nicole said, seeing his smile emerge. She brushed a dusting of snow from her dark hair with a scarlet-mittened hand.

"Joyously," he said, smiling and putting his arm around her waist, drawing her to him. Her 5'4" was still lithe and sinuous. A good fit for his medium height.

They reached the little pond, breathing out clouds of steam. They laughed at the stiff-legged gaggle of geese floundering on the frozen surface.

"We don't spend enough time here," he said. "The beauty just fills me with awe sometimes."

"Oh yes, *cheri*," she said, looking up at him, noticing the gray in his dark, thinning hair and his hazel eyes, behind his glasses that his smile always touched. Those quick intelligent eyes. The way she caught him looking at his body in the mirror, pulling in his stomach. As if his chunky build could make a difference. Men. She squeezed his gloved hand in hers. "I am sorry I have been so busy."

"I know it's been hard since you took over Witten's. I couldn't run a company with two thousand employees." He gave a small laugh. "I don't see how you do it." He watched her eyes as she looked up at him. They were frank and stirringly alive. "I know you love it. But between my teaching and your work, it seems like we never have enough time together."

"Yes. It has been hard. But at least you can come to New York for the weekend, or I can come here. I love you, *cheri*," she said, squeezing his hand again.

Nicole was American by birth. She had been raised in New York. But she was French by descent and preference, a scion of one of the most important families in France. A family with whom she now had little contact. They had met when Jonathan helped Simon Aaron save his great art auction house, Witten's, from an attempted takeover.

She turned to him and put her hand to his face. As he turned towards her, she stood on tiptoes and kissed him. He took her into his arms. She moved her head and sunlight bathed her elegant features. He felt a warmth touch him inside, even in the cold. Her foreign-bred qualities were a continuing source of fascination to him, some exotic grace note to his days.

"I'm glad the winter break's almost here. Let's try to get away," he said.

"Perhaps we can. It would be wonderful." But there was an element of hesitation in her voice.

He was proud of this dark-haired, handsome woman and how four years ago she had leveraged Simon into making her the chief executive officer of Witten's. And how she had grown it and shaped it into something even more important.

How even though she was wealthy, she wanted to work, to achieve something. He loved the way she thought, how she cut through things to their core. The range of her mind. And most of all, that she loved him. The last thought was warm in the crystal cool air.

It was worth it, he mused silently. To have someone to share a morning like this with. Even if he had to give up the adventure of not knowing what new woman would appear in his life tomorrow or the day after. He had never forgotten the excitement he used to feel, wondering who would share his bed that night. It had been fun. This was just better. He drew his coat tighter around him.

He thought back on how he had always been dating two or three beautiful young women at a time then, before he met Nicole. How—what would you say?—stimulating it had been. How his law school colleagues had been amused. Probably even envious, judging by some of their remarks. And how his reputation at the law school, at least among his colleagues' wives, had improved over the last few years. Somehow they just didn't seem to appreciate all those different young women. They had no idea how boring those young girls had been, at least out of bed, or they might have been more sympathetic. The thought amused him. It was better this way.

"What are you thinking, *cheri*?"

"Oh, only how wonderful it would be to go someplace warm and just be together. Maybe the Caribbean. St. Maarten?"

"How has your teaching been?" she asked diverting him. "Are you still unhappy?"

He shrugged. "You know how it is. Teaching's great, but it just isn't as stimulating as deal-making used to be. In a way, the Fernaud thing four years ago kind of ruined me. It was exciting. Teaching just isn't. But life goes on." His voice had a shadow of resignation. "I'm okay. This joint MBA/JD class I'm giving at the business school is interesting. The kids are really bright. They keep me on my toes."

He grabbed her hand playfully. "Let's not talk about anything as mundane as teaching. Not on a morning like this." He turned back towards the old house and pointed over the new tracks they had made in the snowy field. "I'll cook you a first-class breakfast if you'll sleep with me. Want to race?"

Chapter three

"Warren, I'm glad we could find time to meet." It had been difficult to arrange. "We'll need to work closely on Arthur's estate."

Mimi Aaron was sitting in her apartment with Warren Hovington, the departed Arthur DeRuk's art dealer. His attitude appeared a bit stiff. His thin mouth, below a straight aquiline nose, was set in a mild censure. Perhaps not a censure so much as lack of interest.

The snowstorm had passed, and Mimi's apartment with its big windows and high ceiling was filled with light and air. Fresh blossoms caught the yellows and blues of the décor and filled the air with their fragrance. Central Park spread out below them, across Fifth Avenue, like a blank white canvas awaiting an artist's touch.

"Can I give you some coffee?" Her hand moved in a delicate arc of inquiry.

"No, thank you. I'm afraid I haven't too much time." He glanced at his thin gold watch. "I have a board meeting in an hour." He shifted in his armchair and crossed his long legs.

"Warren, I didn't know you were into business. Other than the gallery, I mean."

"Oh. No. This is a charity. I'm on the board of P.E.T.A."

"Really? I've heard of it, but I can't recall what they do."

"We're committed to protecting animals. From research and the like. You wouldn't believe what goes on." His voice carried a timbre that surprised her. The impression she had of him had always been one of suppressed control. His blue hooded eyes never seemed to warm to any subject. Now they were eager. "It's unbelievably cruel. They blind rabbits to test deodorant. Deodorant!" He shuddered as he sat in the warm sunlight.

"Your commitment's wonderful. I had no idea you were so involved."

"Yes. But Mimi, I really don't have long." He glanced down at his watch again. "Can we go on?"

Mimi nodded. Warren Hovington's tall, thin frame never seemed to be in repose for long. She got immediately to the point.

"Warren, I've never been an executor before and I'm not entirely sure what has to be done."

"Yes. It's quite complicated."

He recrossed his long legs and sat back in his chair, regarding her with the fixed gaze of his guarded eyes. "I don't know why Arthur burdened you with this." He shrugged. "In any case, I brought over several things I think you'll need." He retrieved his leather portfolio from the coffee table and pulled out several sheets of paper. "Here's an inventory of all of Arthur's pieces that I have at the gallery or that I collected from his apartment." He passed across several typed sheets of paper. "As you can see, I've described each piece, including the series number on the piece if it's a sculpture or part of a multiple." He pointed at the papers with a delicate manicured finger.

"Sorry?"

Hovington's thin lips tightened. "Mimi, you've collected art for years. I'm surprised."

"Yes, but I've never collected sculpture." Her voice had a defensive note. She wasn't used to being lectured. "Really only oils and works on paper. I know lithographs and the like are done in a series, but I didn't realize it was true of sculpture." She smiled at him to bridge the small awkwardness, although the smile didn't rise to her eyes.

"Only cast sculpture," he continued. "Arthur did series of twelve. Occasionally he did series of eight. There are also maquettes, miniatures done as studies to prepare for larger works. As you can see, I have them all listed for you," he said, pointing to the papers again. "Page three, I believe."

"Good. Thank you. I also think we should discuss your fees." She had no idea if that was right, but it seemed obvious since she was responsible for the money in Arthur DeRuk's estate.

"Just my usual charges. Fifty percent of the sales price of each piece. And of course, any out-of-pocket costs I incur in the sales process or as art executor of the estate. I also believe we must prepare a catalog raissone. If you agree, then I would expect to be paid for my time at my usual rate as a consultant."

Her eyes darkened. "Do you really think that's necessary, Warren? Can we afford it?"

"I don't believe we can afford not to. I can defer my fees if necessary. We have to guard the estate against forgery. There must be one place to establish with certainty the veracity of any DeRuk piece. No one will ever be in a better position to prepare the catalog of all of Arthur's work than I am. After all, I have been his dealer for years, and no one knows his work better." He steepled his fingers in a celebration of expertise.

"You should also know that I will be making a claim against the estate," he said, his hooded blue eyes finding hers. "Arthur owed me several hundred thousand dollars, which with interest amounts to well over four hundred thousand dollars today."

He reached for a piece of paper from his portfolio case with some calculations on it and spent a moment reviewing them. Then he handed it to her.

"Oh, my," she said uncertainly. "And Arthur owed me over two hundred thousand, as you know. That will mean the estate will be quite illiquid."

Hovington's eyes stayed on hers. "Yes, that is unfortunate, but I advanced Arthur a great deal of money for his living expenses." Hovington made a tching sound, the nostrils flaring in his aquiline nose. "Arthur was so extravagant. But, of course, my advances were secured by his art works. I need the money back."

"Weren't four pieces from the estate just sold at auction?" Mimi asked, sifting through the papers Hovington had given to her. "They brought in a good deal of money, didn't they?"

"Well, yes, but unfortunately I had to make refunds on three of the pieces that were sold. I'll send you the lot numbers and descriptions together with my canceled checks. You'll find them on the inventory. As to the fourth piece, I withheld my commission and applied the balance to the amount due me from the estate." He glanced at his watch.

"But you need to look at the good side," he said, his

voice timbre now buoyant. "It was a very successful sale. There were record prices set for Arthur's works. I was very pleased."

Sunlight shaded to shadow across the room's blue and yellow pastels.

"I don't understand why there were refunds on three of the pieces," Mimi said, the concern sounding in her voice. "Where will the estate get the money to operate? Will there be more sales soon?"

"Well, there were irregularities, and I felt it was in the estate's best interest to make the refunds." The thin mouth pressed into a smile.

"Irregularities?"

"It's really too complicated to go into right now." He looked again at his watch and stirred in his chair. "Perhaps we can discuss it at our next meeting. But I felt it had to be done. You know, Mimi, as Arthur's art executor, I'm responsible for selling his art and timing the sales. After all, I lost money too since the sales didn't go through," he said, brushing at his razor-creased pants leg.

"Unfortunately, there's no money at this time to transfer to you," he continued. "I don't anticipate any further auction sales in the next several months. We've got to resist injuring Arthur's reputation by flooding the market. If there's too much supply, I'm concerned with the price his work will bring. You have to trust me on this. You know I cared about Arthur too."

As he spoke he rose and gathered up his leather portfolio. He extended his hand in a practiced act.

"But, I really have to be on my way. I have so many things I need to attend to. I'll keep you advised."

Mimi rose to take Hovington's outstretched hand. "Of course, Warren. I'm just concerned how I'll be able to handle the estate. I'm already being contacted by some of the beneficiaries asking for money. Please do your best."

Mimi sat back down after she closed the door. The sunlight brightened as a cloud passed away from the sun. Her glance took in the snowy park as she reflected on the conversation. She loved Central Park when it had a cover of new snow.

She wondered if being Arthur's executor was going to be a problem. She certainly didn't understand most of what Warren was talking about. And the way he constantly looked at his watch was so unpleasant. Arthur deserved better.

Below, a horse and carriage traced two lines in the new snow. "Maybe I need to find someone I can trust to help me," she said, watching the horse-drawn lines extending across naked white space.

Chapter four

The room was dark. The strobing flashes bounced off the mirrors and gave the dancing forms an old-time jerky movie motion. The sound was almost visible.

She was sitting with her friend at one of the small tables away from the dance floor. Both of them were in their late twenties and veterans. They were drinking cosmopolitans.

Myacura Ishii's long black hair hung straight and lacquered around a face set off by exotic-looking dark eyes. The thin red jersey dress she wore accentuated her small, pointy breasts and long legs. She was shaking her head angrily. The motion made her hair sway, catching the light. They were leaning towards each other and almost shouting to be heard.

"And you let him do that to you?" her friend asked.

"Hey. You know. Men like it that way. He was a lawyer. I wanted to see him again." She spoke like someone who knew her subject.

"Did it feel good?" Her friend was clearly curious. There was no judgement in her voice. "I've never done it like that."

"Not really. Men are such pigs."

That drew a knowing nod.

"Besides, we were both high."

"What?"

"Nose candy. He had some good stuff."

"Yeah?"

A young man in a tee shirt and blue jeans approached their table. They stared him off.

"Shit. There's no one here tonight," Ishii said, changing the subject. "I'm bored. Have you got any pills?"

"Ecstasy."

"Let's have some." She tapped on the table with a long red-lacquered nail.

Her friend shuffled through her purse and passed a small pill across. Ishii downed it with a swallow of her cosmopolitan.

"Has he called you?" her friend asked, returning to the prior discussion.

"No, the asshole."

Ishii compressed her lips into a thin scarlet line. "I saw him," she continued. "Last night. At a restaurant opening. He was with another woman. He didn't see me. She was hanging all over him." Ishii paused. "She had a face like a horse. And she was wearing a ring."

"He's married?"

"He said he was single."

"The bastard. Damn them. Are they all like that? I went out with a guy for almost four months before he told me he was married. I wanted to cut his balls off."

Ishii gave a snort. Her friend looked over at her.

"What're you going to do?" she asked.

"Maybe I'll give his horsey little wife a call. Leave her a nice message. You know. Or maybe I'll just cut off his balls."

Her friend gave a thin, uncertain laugh. Myacura Ishii didn't smile.

The cab ride home wasn't that long. But it was long enough for Ishii to reflect on the lawyer.

The heater in the cab was broken. The driver huddled in front in his heavy jacket. Ishii didn't notice, absorbed in her thoughts. Her lips were a scarlet gash. Streetlights changed her face from darkness to light and back again.

Why was this happening to her? Why was she being used like this? Her fingers curled into a fist, the blood-red nails biting into her palm.

She wanted to hurt him. She knew she wanted to hurt him. Twist out his guts. The street lights strobed faster now.

She hated him. Just like she had hated Arthur DeRuk.

Chapter five

"No," Jonathan said. He pushed his glasses up on his nose and shifted his body to a more comfortable position, the phone cradled to his ear. He was sitting in his small, crowded office at the law school with his feet up on his desk among the stacks of year-old law reviews. He had been staring out the window, watching the clouds and thinking about Nicole, when Simon Aaron's call interrupted him.

" 'No' is not an answer." The voice was wheedling. It was how Simon sounded when he wanted something. " 'Yes.' Now that's an answer."

"Simon, I'm busy with classes. I'm working on a paper to present in January, and Nicole and I want to get away over the term break." He turned away from the window and shifted the phone to the other ear. "She's been working far too hard." It was a pointed accusation since she worked for Simon.

"But Mimi's in trouble." It was a game with Simon.

Jonathan always thought he would have had a bright future in Yiddish theatre.

"I never met Mimi," Jonathan responded. "You never invited me over for dinner when I was your lawyer. Besides, it's been three years since the divorce. Come on. I know you. Why the sudden concern? What's in it for you?"

"Well, yeah." It was a grudging admission. "Mimi did offer to give me a voting agreement on the Witten's shares she got in the divorce if I helped her out. But that's not why I'm doing it," he said quickly. "She was my wife, for goodness sakes." Simon's tone carried wounded dignity. Jonathan had hit close to the mark.

Witten's was the love of Simon Aaron's life, the auction house Jonathan had helped him buy when he was practicing corporate law at Whiting & Pierce, before he had returned to teach at Harvard. And the one he'd helped him save four years ago when Simon's old rival, Vincent Rollins, had made a run at the company. Where he and Nicole had met. "*Cheri. . .*" her voice echoed.

"Simon, have you forgotten? The last time I played detective it was a disaster. I was so busy tripping over the wrong end of the stick that it was blind luck we got through it. Why me?"

"This isn't some kind of mystery," Simon said in an aggrieved tone. "It's just a little problem with the police. Mimi was in the wrong place at the wrong time."

"So get her a criminal lawyer." Jonathan looked at his feet. One shoe was scuffed. He needed to get them polished.

"It's not that simple."

"Why?"

"Uh—she thinks you're some kind of genius."

"You're kidding me. How could she have gotten that

idea? I don't even know her."

"I may have accidentally given her that impression," Simon said, his voice spinning defensively down the line.

"Simon, you don't do things by accident. Tell me exactly how she got this impression."

"It was during the divorce."

"Yes?"

"I guess I was trying to explain to her how difficult the auction business is and why she should sell me her stock."

"Uh-huh."

"Maybe I told her about the problems we were having, and how it could have wiped us out if it hadn't been for you."

"So you played it up to get Mimi to sell out to you at a low price."

"You might say that." He sounded rather like a small boy caught with his hand in the cookie jar.

"She didn't bite?"

"No."

"And now you want me to bail you out."

"Well, I wouldn't put it that way. You're my friend." He brightened. "Besides, Nicole likes me. After all, I made her managing director of Witten's."

"Yeah. Right."

As Jonathan recalled, it had not been an altogether magnanimous gesture on Simon's part. In fact, Nicole had taken him to the cleaners. He smiled to himself, shifting his feet on the desk and tipping some law reviews over onto the floor. "Damn," he muttered, removing his feet to lean over to retrieve them. He sneezed from the dust he raised.

"*Gezundheit*," Simon said.

"Look, Simon, I like you, although for the life of me,

I don't know why. You aren't exactly the cuddliest cub in the zoo. In fact, you're usually a roaring asshole."

"I can be a little gruff sometimes, maybe. But help me out with this, will you?"

"Simon, I'm just too busy."

"I'll give you five percent of the shares in that winery I invested in in Santa Ynez."

"Zager? World class pinot?" Jonathan recalled the blind tasting he had attended two months ago.

"Yeah."

Jonathan took off his glasses. "Hold it, Simon. Any debt on the winery?"

"Nope. Now do I have your attention?" The wheedling voice had been replaced by a businesslike tone.

"You'll transfer the shares to me up front, free and clear?"

"Okay."

"Send me the financial statements?"

"Sure."

Jonathan fell silent for a moment, considering. It sounded interesting. God knows he needed some stimulation.

"Will it take much time?"

"No way. Just give her some advice." Simon sounded earnest, and he wanted to believe him.

Jonathan swung his glasses by the stem. "I'll have to talk to Nicole, but I think I may be able to fit you in. As I've always said, I can't be bought—but I can be rented."

Chapter six

Warren Hovington was sitting in his office above the gallery, staring at his manicured hands on the desk in front of him. This was a call he really didn't want to make. It had been a perfectly nice afternoon. The sunlight through the big window warmed his back. He sighed as he raised a hand to pick up the phone. Better get it over with. Things were getting pretty tight since Arthur's death.

"Essame. This is Warren Hovington."

"Asshole!" The phone banged down.

He pressed the redial button. Essame Quinn had always been volatile. Hovington could envision the rough mouth behind the broad, unkempt beard.

"Don't hang up. Listen."

"Why?"

"Because you need me."

"Fuck you."

"Be that as it may, you still need me. I have a proposition for you."

"Now that DeRuk is dead and you're hung out to dry, you think I'll come crawling back to your gallery when you crook your little finger? After what you and that little prick did to me? Go stick it up your ass."

There was a trace of dust on the phone. Hovington wiped at it with his thumb. "It was only business. I told you then."

"Only business!" Quinn shouted, anger riding his voice. Hovington thought he heard a glass crash against a wall. "It cost me my marriage. My fucking house got foreclosed on. I wish I could have gotten my hands on you."

"Essame," Hovington said with exaggerated calmness, "DeRuk made me drop you. He would have quit the gallery if I hadn't."

Quinn exploded again. "So what?"

"He was my biggest artist. His work sold for two or three times what yours did, and a lot more of it sold." The dust smudging his thumb irritated him. He vowed to fire the cleaning woman. He crossed his long legs and cradled the phone to reach for a tissue.

"Look, I told you not to badmouth DeRuk." He wiped his thumb clean. "Why did you talk to that *Times* art critic? Did you have to call DeRuk a fraud?"

"The shit was a fraud. He couldn't draw a straight line. Art. That makes me laugh. He was a clown."

"DeRuk was furious."

"What the fuck do I care? I told the truth. My dog knew more about art. And he was smarter." Quinn sounded drunk.

"Don't you want to hear what I have to say? I know things haven't been going well for you. I can change that."

Quinn went quiet. The words came reluctantly. "Let's

hear it. But make it quick. I get nauseated talking to you."

"Essame, you're a great talent," Hovington said, rubbing the side of his long nose. "I've always told you that. Your work reaches down inside and wrings out emotion from people. It moves them. You can't let it wither away."

Quinn grunted.

"I'll make the same deal with you I made with Arthur DeRuk. I'll loan you money on each painting you deliver to me, depending on the size. You pay me back plus interest when the picture sells."

"How much do you make?" Quinn sounded interested.

"On what?"

"Commissions."

"Oh, I'll get the usual fifty percent of the sales price. But I'll work with you to raise your prices. You saw what I did for DeRuk."

Another, more interested grunt, a gathering of his ego.

"You'll be the gallery's number one artist. I'll guarantee you a one-man show every two years and arrange a one-man show out of town every year. We'll see about Europe."

"Go on."

"I'll manage your funds without cost, just like I did for DeRuk. I'll make sure you get enough to live on so you can work. You create, I'll take care of the business end."

"I'll think about it." The phone slammed down again.

Hovington smiled as he replaced the receiver.

Chapter seven

"Professor Franklin."

"Jonathan. Please."

"Jonathan, I appreciate your coming all this way to help me."

The older woman was small and elegant. No more than 5'3". Her natural silver-gray hair was stylishly cut. The cashmere twin set looked deep and soft, and the color caught a hint of her eyes. The single strand of pearls around her neck was exquisite. At the moment Mimi Aaron had a bemused smile on her face.

"Mrs. Aaron . . ."

"No," she said, leaning forward and putting her hand on his arm. "If I'm to call you Jonathan, then you will have to call me Mimi." She smiled up at him. "Please come in. We can sit in the living room. It's so nice when the sun shines."

She showed him to an armchair. The flowers in the apartment were massed to reflect the pastels and blues of the décor. They seemed to draw in the snowy expanse of Central Park and make it part of the room. His eye caught a Chagall oil through the doorway into the dining room.

"Can I get you something?" she asked. Jonathan was struck by her grace, the way she moved. Nicole was quick and efficient. More economical in her movements.

"No, thanks." The more he had thought about his discussion with Simon, the uneasier he had become. What must this woman expect of him?

"I'm not sure I can help you, and to be honest, I'm not even sure why I'm here. I'm a law professor. Simon must have terribly exaggerated what happened at Witten's a few years ago." He spoke more quickly than he had intended. He shifted his position in the armchair and fiddled with his wire-rimmed glasses.

"Jonathan, I was married to Simon for 28 years." Her eyes captured her smile. Green. Or were they gray? "Do you think I don't know him? When he wants something he can charm the spots off a leopard, but he doesn't always tell the truth." She chuckled. "I knew exactly what he was doing when he told me about what happened at Witten's, and I didn't believe a word of it. But I wanted your help. I may have exaggerated my—what to say?— peril with the police. But even then I know Simon well enough to know the only way to get him to convince you to help me was to offer him the voting agreement on my Witten's stock."

"Why would you do that?"

She rose and wandered to one of the floor-to-ceiling windows overlooking the park. She seemed to gather her arguments for a moment. Then she turned back to him. He was surprised at how her presence seemed to fill the room.

"First, it didn't cost me anything. I wanted Simon to

have the voting rights. It will make him feel better and he'll make the value of the stock go up. He loves Witten's. And in a peculiar way, I still love him." She made a delicate gesture with her left hand. Jonathan noticed the large diamond she still wore. "So you see, I got you, I made Simon happy and it was free. In fact, I'll make money. I usually get what I want." Somehow her statement wasn't a challenge. Simply a fact. Perhaps it was because her eyes were still smiling.

Jonathan took in this woman he had never met before. She would have been a formidable adversary even for Simon Aaron. "If you still care about him, why did you get a divorce?"

"I'm 57 years old and rich beyond the dreams of Croesus." She resumed her seat, facing him across the corner of the coffee table. He noticed the way she folded her hands in her lap, like nesting doves. "Simon went off years ago with his mistress."

The statement startled him. He blushed. There had been rumors about Simon, but there were some questions you didn't ask. He opened his mouth. "Ah—"

"Come on, Jonathan," she interrupted, leaning forward and putting her hand on his arm. "I mean Witten's. I love art and I love the art scene. But with Simon it's different. It absorbs him like I haven't for years. Like no woman could. And I believe if you can't compete, you get out of the game." Her eyes darkened for a moment as she withdrew her hand. "In any case. . . " she said with a shrug.

"I . . . " Jonathan began.

She interrupted him. "I'm sorry, Jonathan, but I'm dying for a cup of coffee. Are you sure I can't get you some?"

"Sure, if you're having some."

"Decaffeinated or regular?"

"Whatever you're making."

She rose and went through the dining room to the kitchen beyond. He heard her murmur something to someone he couldn't see.

She returned, followed almost immediately by a middle-aged Latina carrying a tray with a silver coffee service. The woman set the tray on the coffee table and started to pour. "Jonathan, this is Maria," Mimi said. "I wouldn't know what to do without her." The Latina woman smiled without lifting her eyes and nodded as she finished pouring. She made a tiny almost-curtsy and withdrew.

"Cream?" Mimi asked.

She looked at Jonathan over her coffee cup, and she liked what she saw. This middle-aged man, a little disheveled in his tweed jacket, of medium height, slightly chunky, with quick intelligent eyes below a receding hairline. But more than that, she noticed, when he smiled, he smiled with his hazel eyes in a way his glasses couldn't conceal. She'd chosen well.

"Simon and I are friends. Probably better friends now, Jonathan, than when we were married." Light and shadows played in the room as clouds toyed with the winter sun. "He calls every few days to make sure I'm all right. And when he's in town, he stops by. He even spends the night sometimes."

"I can understand all that, Mimi. It makes sense. But what doesn't make sense is that if you didn't believe all Simon's stuff, why me? Simon told me your fingerprints were on the syringe that was used. He said the police were suspicious. I advised Simon to get you a criminal lawyer."

"Nonsense." She said it firmly. "I'm not afraid of the police. I didn't do anything. I just don't trust them to sort out Arthur." She replaced her coffee cup in its saucer and set it on the table.

"Arthur?"

"Arthur DeRuk, the man who died. Arthur was a great artist." She glanced at a photo on the side table. Jonathan followed her glance. The man in the photo was middle-aged, with dark hair and dark eyes. Almost gypsy-like. The pose was informal. He was wearing swimming trunks topped by an open shirt. Some vacation spot.

"But, to say the least, he was complex," Mimi continued. "For all Arthur's flaws, we were very close." She looked towards the photo again. "He even named me executor of his estate, and I'm not comfortable about it. What I need from you is a good legal mind to help me. Someone I can depend on to give me sound advice. More than just legal advice. Strategic advice. If I want a criminal lawyer, I don't need Simon. I have money and friends." Her voice gained certainty. "I wanted you."

Jonathan looked confused. "I still don't understand." He shifted uneasily in his chair.

"It's because of what Simon didn't say about you when you worked with him on restructuring Witten's."

That's a strange reason, Jonathan thought.

"Simon is intolerant of his advisors, you know. He vents."

An ironic smile touched Jonathan's face. "Tell me about it," he said, remembering back.

"He bad-mouths them all, even those he's used or perhaps misused for years. You included, when you were his lawyer." She lifted her cup and sipped her coffee. "He didn't say a bad thing about you when you were helping him with Witten's. He may have even muttered something nice under his breath once or twice, although I'm not positive." Her smile blossomed again. "That said worlds to me. Simon was as good as I've ever seen at finding the best for what he needed. It was a talent. And I thought I needed the same thing." She stopped as if she had just thought of something she was curious about. "By the way, exactly what did Simon offer you to help me?"

"Five percent of Zager Vineyards."

"Ah!"

"What do you mean, 'Ah'?"

"Oh, nothing at all." She started to hurry on.

"No, really," he interrupted, his eyes quick. "What do you mean?"

"I only heard Simon muttering about Zager. I didn't really pay attention. I don't know anything more."

That gave him pause.

"I need someone who's smart and clever," she went on. "Who has the stature to circulate among the people in Arthur's world. Someone they'll talk to if I introduce you."

His thoughts lurched from the vineyards, back to what Mimi was saying. He watched her gather her hands together, dove soft. She had remarkable hands.

"It's possible Arthur may have committed suicide. He was a recovering drug addict and an alcoholic. He was terribly hurt when Rufus was kidnapped."

"Who's Rufus?"

"His pug." She managed a smile. "He loved him. He could play with that puppy for hours. You should have seen them down on the floor. He lavished attention on him. No man who loved an animal like that could be all bad, could he?" Her eyes found his.

"Mimi, I don't understand why you care. Why are you going to so much trouble?" He lifted his coffee cup to his lips. It was cold.

Wordlessly, she rose and went over to a vase full of

yellow tulips. She put her hand behind one. "Jonathan, do you like flowers?"

"Yes, of course. Yours are beautiful."

"Why do you like them?"

"I guess because they give me a sense of joy. I've never really thought about it."

She nodded and sat down again. "They add something to your life."

"Yes."

"You see, that's why I care. There aren't many people I treasure. Arthur was not altogether a good person. He had a vile temper and was wholly self-absorbed. He could be ruthless. But he also could be charming."

"You make him sound like Simon."

She ignored that. "He engaged my mind. How do you grow without that? He was a rare person. Good or bad, he was real. And as his executor, I feel I have a responsibility."

Tears veiled her eyes. Jonathan's lawyerly instincts kicked in. She seemed to be overreacting.

"Arthur's death may have been an accident, but I don't think so. He was coming around. He would come over here and we would just talk for hours. He liked to sit right where you're sitting. We made plans. He was going back into rehabilitation. He was excited about a new concept he had for his art. God knows he had enough enemies. Arthur stirred up a lot of emotion. I could name two or three people who hated him. And every one of them is as complex and clever, and as vicious as Arthur could be."

"Vicious?"

"Oh, yes."

As he set down his coffee cup, Jonathan wondered just what he had signed on for.

chapter eight

He was sitting in his office looking out over the dealership floor. Normally the sight of all the shiny new cars jazzed him. Not today.

"Damn artists!"

Walter Demian was in a foul mood.

"Paid good money. No consideration whatsoever. He didn't even have the courtesy to respond. Well—we'll see about that."

He liked to get his own way. Walter Demian was a big man. Six feet and almost 300 pounds. He caught a glimpse of himself on the television set that ran a loop of all his commercials. I'd really better start doing some exercise, he thought. I'm starting to look like a hog. Can't have that.

Demian was muttering to himself as he wrote the follow-up letter. He would be damned if he wasn't going to get a reply. He was just as good as any other collector. Exactly who did these people think they were? He tapped the end of the ballpoint pen against his teeth. He noticed one of his salesmen down on the floor shaking hands with a skinny man in farm clothes and smiling broadly. Slapping him on the back as he led him towards the back to the sales manager's office. "Where was I?" he said aloud to the empty room.

That DeRuk sculpture was the most expensive piece of art he'd ever bought. But he couldn't resist a bargain. He didn't get to New York all that often. It was a long way from Tulsa with no direct flights. Well, now it was time to give the sculpture away to the museum.

It had been a bang-up year at his car dealerships, what with the new models and all. Damn government would suck him dry again unless he got a big deduction. The very thought of it made his lips sag into a frown. And it was already November. It had been June when he first wrote to DeRuk.

The sculpture was worth five times what he'd paid for it three years ago. His accountant told him he could get a deduction for the whole thing if he gave it to the museum. And he wouldn't even be taxed on the appreciation. That appealed to him. He would almost make more by giving it away than by selling it. Make money by giving it away. He liked that.

And he might get that board seat at the museum he had been angling for over the last two years. They never took him seriously, just because he wore a cowboy hat on television and acted like a rube. Well, those fools didn't know how to make money, at least not the kind of money he was making.

People trusted folks on those big charity boards. Publicity wouldn't hurt either. He opened a drawer and made a note on his pad. Better talk to that publicity gal he was thinking about hiring. The one with the big tits.

The museum was anxious to get this piece of art. He didn't want them to cool off. But he needed the right appraiser. That's what he wanted to know out of this DeRuk fella.

It was good to be an astute art collector. And generous. Don't forget generous. He'd make a good board member at the museum.

He was almost gleeful now, but that made him even madder when he remembered the asshole artist who didn't even have the courtesy to respond to his last letter. His big hand slashed his name across the bottom of the letter.

He read it over. Damn right. He made it pretty clear that he wasn't happy. This should get him some action.

He folded the letter, addressed an envelope, stamped it and threw it into his outbox.

He had no idea of the events he had set in motion.

Chapter nine

"Simon!"

"Simon!"

Jonathan was shouting into the telephone. He was standing in the hallway of Nicole's apartment next to a small oil painting of the booksellers beside the Seine. He never understood what Nicole saw in that picture.

"Are you there, Simon? I can hardly hear you. Where are you? It sounds like you're in a wind tunnel."

"Hold on," Simon shouted above the noise, "I just got off the plane." Simon glanced back at his new private jet, a Gulfstream G-5. "I'm going inside."

There were a few moments of silence on the line.

"Who's this?"

"Simon, it's Jonathan. Where are you?"

"Teterborough. We just came in from London. Did you see Mimi?"

"Yes. I just left her." Jonathan realized he was still shouting. He lowered his voice. "We met for an hour. Are you coming into New York?"

"I'll be there in about an hour and a half. Do you want to sit down?"

"Yeah. I think it'd be a good idea," Jonathan said. "I'm at Nicole's apartment. Do you want to come here or do you want to meet at the Carlyle?" It was one of Simon's favorite places. He maintained an apartment there.

"Let's do the Carlyle. I'll call you from the car."

The Café Carlyle was quiet at four in the afternoon. They had a table in the corner under the music-themed murals. Jonathan realized there was no one else in the room. "Boy, this is quiet," he said, turning towards Simon. "I didn't know they served tea here. I've only been here at night to see Bobby Short."

"They don't. I asked them if they'd mind letting us use the room." Simon had clout.

Jonathan tugged his tie loose and shed his tweed jacket as Simon settled his round, well-tailored body into the booth beside him. Simon's dark blue suit with the thinnest of red stripes was distinctive and beautifully cut. Savile Row, Jonathan guessed. The tailors had worked wonders with his 5'4" frame.

"How was London?"

"Cold. How's Nicole?" He didn't wait for an answer. Typical Simon. "Send her my love. She's doing a fabulous job at Witten's. I wasn't sure this shift of headquarters to New York was going to work out, but so far it looks great. She's one hell of a lady."

"That she is," Jonathan said.

They were interrupted by a tuxedo-clad waiter. "May I serve your tea, Mr. Aaron," he murmured, bowing slightly toward Simon.

"Please." Simon turned to Jonathan. "I ordered coffee for you." A smile twitched.

"Hey, I never learned to drink tea. Sue me."

It took a few moments of decorous bustle to set out the coffee, tea and trays of small sandwiches and pastries. Simon reached for some pastries and a sliver of an egg salad sandwich. He held the sandwich up and turned it this way and that.

"I never figured out how they could charge so much for so little food. Good thing I'm not hungry. They must have great food cost though," he said, shifting to his business side. "Oh, sorry, go on." He turned his attention to Jonathan. "How was your meeting with Mimi?"

"I was really impressed," Jonathan said, unfolding his starched white napkin and arranging it in his lap. "She's a strong woman. A great heart, and what a wonderful sense of humor." He stopped for a moment to sip his coffee. It tasted really good. "But Simon, she's taking this thing with Arthur DeRuk too lightly. I think she's got hold of a five-foot snake with a three-foot stick."

Jonathan loved these colorful aphorisms he'd picked up during his years on Wall Street.

"Why?" Simon asked, unwilling to grasp the end of that particular stick.

"She wants to stir things up about DeRuk's death. She has some inkling that it wasn't an accident. It's nuts for her to get into this. With her fingerprints on the syringe, she'd be the prime suspect. She's sticking her head straight into the lion's mouth."

Simon barked out a laugh, fixing Jonathan with a look. "Well, that's Mimi in a nutshell," he said as he wiped a speck of egg salad from the corner of his mouth.

"Simon, you've got to speak to her."

"Oh, no. Not me." Simon shook his head. Jonathan

swore he saw his eyes widen. "You don't know Mimi very well. She's as stubborn as a mule. When she gets her teeth into something, she won't let go. Not for anything. A wonderful woman, but really, really stubborn." He emphasized the word "really." "If you can't convince her, I don't know who can."

Simon chewed thoughtfully, then started again.

"Jonathan. Money isn't an object. Get Perone, Brill involved if you think it'll help. She's not going to back down. I know this woman. Just help her." His voice had a vulnerable quality unusual for him. "Sometimes she gets in over her head. And she's not as strong as she makes out."

His concern was palpable. Maybe he did still care.

Jonathan reached for one of the small pastries. "I'll try. I'll call Frankee Perone if I think she can do anything. Right now I just don't see how an investigator's going to help."

Simon seemed relieved. He shoved his plate aside and reached for the briefcase beside his chair. He took out a large envelope.

"I brought along the financials for Zager Vineyards. You asked for them."

"Nice of you to remember. I'll look them over when I get a chance." Jonathan put the envelope aside.

"Er—could you do it sooner rather than later?"

Jonathan's pastry stopped halfway to his mouth. "Why?"

"I want to talk to you about them."

Jonathan carefully returned the pastry to his plate. There was more to this. And he wasn't going to like it. Not at all.

Chapter ten

"Jonathan, are you awake?"

They had returned to Nicole's apartment on Central Park West late in the evening after dinner and the theatre. It had been one in the morning when they finally got to bed. He didn't really want to move. It was warm and cozy under the covers. Besides, he wasn't a morning person. He opened one eye against the light.

"Kind of," he said sleepily.

"Can I ask you a question?"

He was suddenly wide-awake. He knew that tone. "Sure."

"I need to understand something."

"What?"

"Are there any limitations on our relationship?"

Every nerve in Jonathan's body was now on high alert.

"Er—no. Why are you asking?"

"Because I am 38. We have been together now almost

four years. I need to understand where we are going. How you feel about me."

"You know I love you," Jonathan said, burrowing down into the blankets against his uneasy feeling. "What more do you want?" He turned over on his side to face her.

"How do you feel about marriage?" The big M word.

"I guess it's okay, but our relationship is so great. I've never felt closer to anyone. Why should we change something wonderful and exciting?"

"I may want to have a child at some point. It is important to me."

"It is? You never said anything about a child before." He felt defensive. No. Terrified.

"It has become more important. I need to understand how you feel."

"I'm—I'm just not sure. A child. This is a complete surprise. I've never thought about it." A child at 51. "I just don't know."

He kicked back the covers and rolled into a sitting position on the side of the bed, his back turned to Nicole. He fumbled on the nightstand for his glasses. He needed his glasses to think clearly. Or maybe to hide behind.

"I believe that we need to think about this, Jonathan. Let us think while I am away in London. I do not wish to push you. I too love our relationship."

Jonathan felt confused and a little angry.

"Do you have to go to London? I was hoping we could get away. I feel like we don't have enough time together."

She reached over and put her hand to his back. Her gray eyes softened. "I would love to, but I have meetings at Witten's I cannot reschedule. I have not been to London for a month. I am sorry, *cheri*."

A sense of dread spread over Jonathan. He could feel the tightening in his chest.

A child. Fifty-one.

Chapter eleven

The breakfast nook in Nicole's apartment was done in a cheery yellow and it was flooded with morning sunlight. Jonathan was less cheerful than his surroundings as he turned over the last page of the financial statement of Zager Vineyards. He took off his glasses and rubbed the bridge of his nose. Then he reached for his cell phone.

"Simon, damn it, you snookered me." Jonathan had finally reached Simon at Mimi's apartment. "These aren't financial statements, they're an obituary. Zager Vineyards lost"—he shifted the papers in front of him—"$120,000 last year. That's apart from the investment in new equipment. The balance sheet stinks. They have a negative net worth. And I own five percent of this mess?"

"But see. No debt. Like I told you. Besides, two hundred acres of land isn't borscht. And you get six cases of wine a year as a dividend."

Simon sounded so innocent Jonathan couldn't suppress a smile. Simon often sank into the vernacular when he played the innocent.

"Simon, stop it."

"No debt," Simon persisted *sotto voce* in a pouting voice.

It was too much. "Simon. You're unbelievable. You used Mimi's problem to suck me in. Not only did you get me to help her out, you laid off this loser on me."

"It's true we have a few problems at Zager," Simon said, "but I look at it as an opportunity."

"What, an opportunity to lose money?"

"Now, now. Don't be so harsh." Simon's voice was almost angelic. "With a little work, your five percent will double in value. Maybe triple."

Jonathan could hear cups rattling in the background and he could picture Simon having breakfast in Mimi's apartment, looking back towards him across the park. He imagined he was smiling in his Cheshire cat kind of way.

"How much money did you have to put in last year?"

"A little bit."

"How little?"

"That's not important," Simon said, avoiding the question. "What is important is that here I am trying to help you make some money. And what do I get? Accusations." Now Simon sounded wounded.

"Simon, have you had acting lessons I don't know about?"

"No need to be snide. So look. You know about wine. And I might point out, whining too." Simon didn't sound in the least bit offended. "Sure, you may have to do a little work. But is it so bad to make another half million dollars for a few hours of your time? I ask you." Simon's pose of bewilderment came across loud and clear.

"My God, are you entering stage left? Let me get this straight. Sweet, rich Simon Aaron is only concerned about his poor, hardworking teacher pal, Jonathan Benjamin Franklin."

"That's it."

"And if I help you fix your business problem, I make what—a half million dollars?"

"Exactly."

"And my pal Simon makes what?"

"Maybe a little more," Simon said, injured innocence suffusing his voice.

"You're unbelievable." Jonathan slumped back in his wooden breakfast chair. "I'll think about it. But I'll get you for this."

"Just remember," Simon added, "here I am, giving you a real honest-to-goodness business problem. You could make money. You could lose it. You should thank me for providing you a little excitement." Jonathan heard Mimi giggle in the background. "Not like all that teaching stuff."

"Okay, okay. What do you want me to do?"

"Nothing. Just spend a couple of days in beautiful, warm California. Drink some wine. Take Nicole with you even. She'll get a kick out of it."

"I can't. She's got to go to London. On your business. What do I have to do in California?"

"Go out and see Dastel Zager. Just a second." He put his hand over the telephone. "Thank you, Mimi," Jonathan heard him say in a muffled voice. Then he started up again. "He's a good guy. Old college buddy. See if you can figure out how to protect our investment." He emphasized the word "our." "You can use the plane. But let's do it soon, before Day asks us for any more money." Jonathan noticed the plural.

"Just what I need right now. Something else on my plate. Isn't Mimi enough? Thank goodness *that* situation hasn't gotten any worse."

"At least the wine will be good," Simon said.

Chapter twelve

Lt. Julian Wayne was having a bad day. His usually short temper was not improved by his cold, making his eyes water and stuffing up his nose. This cold had come on suddenly. He had been fine last night. Now he was sneezing and blowing. He hated winter colds. He felt like he had a fever. He could hardly taste his cigarette. His desk was littered with tissues and cold medicines in addition to the ever-present cardboard cup of cold coffee.

Inspector Tritter took one look and knew he was in the wrong place at the wrong time. "Lieutenant," he said, trying not to poke the dragon. He was standing sideways in the door, presenting the smallest possible target. It was chilly. Wayne must have the thermostat cranked way down.

What he got was a bleary-eyed stare. "What?" Wayne said in an irritated voice.

"Er, here's the lab report on that guy that died from the drug overdose over on the East Side. That artist." He held the thin sheath of papers out in front of him.

"They took their damn time. Give it to me." He glared at the pages as he turned them. He took a drag on his cigarette and coughed.

"Okay. Died between midnight and 8 a.m. Drug overdose." Wayne held the page up closer to his face. He opened the drawer of his desk, pulled out a pair of reading glasses and perched them on his nose. Then he sneezed. He fumbled for a tissue and blew his red nose before turning back to the document.

"Shit," he said, putting the report down among the clutter on his desk. "The stuff left in the syringe was almost pure heroin. No wonder he overdosed." His thick fingers drummed on the desk top. "Someone maybe injected him and set it up to look accidental. I don't like it. Get me the file. We need to talk to that woman who found him. That socialite who thought she was such hot shit, what's her name?" He remembered those gray-green eyes. "Her prints were all over the syringe." He grabbed for a tissue again and blew his nose. "Damn." He reached for a jar of Vaseline and smeared it on.

Tritter nodded. Wayne could easily tear him a new one when he was in this kind of mood.

"Get her in here. And do a background on her and this guy DeRuk."

"Jonathan, it's Mimi."

He had just finished breakfast and was out in Central Park walking it off. Snow drifted down in damp clumps, sticking to his eyelashes. The bare trees danced to their own inner music. He was bundled up against the cold, a seeping cold that seemed to get inside his clothes now that he was standing still. He had tugged off his glove to answer the incessant ringing of his cell phone, and now his hand was red and starting to sting. He pulled his muffler tighter around his neck and hunched forward.

"I just got a call from the police," Mimi said. "They want to talk to me again."

"Is there a problem?" A gust of cold wind blew snow into his face. He turned aside and tugged at his muffler again.

"No, but that Lieutenant Wayne just wants to do a routine follow-up, they said. But I thought you might want to come with me if you have time. You might learn something about Arthur. Do you think he'd like some flowers?"

"What?"

"Some lovely daffodils. They were just delivered."

"No, I meant who?"

"Lieutenant Wayne."

"I don't think so. Mimi, can you hang on a second? I've got to put my glove back on. My hand's going to drop off."

"Oh, dear. I'm sorry. Are you outside? You must be freezing. Would you like me to call you back?"

"No, it's okay. I'm just taking a walk." A young woman, bundled up to her nose, brushed past him and stared. "I'll come with you to see Wayne." The wind picked up. He was anxious to finish, but he had a concern. "Mimi, you know there's no such thing as a 'routine follow-up.' "

"Of course I do. But I didn't do anything wrong."

"When are you going in?"

"Tomorrow morning. Can you join me for breakfast? I know just the place."

"I'd love to. But Mimi, are you sure you don't want to take a lawyer?"

She laughed.

"I have one, don't I?"

Chapter thirteen

It was just after nine. Jonathan rose as Mimi came to the small table he was guarding in the busy patisserie. It was a beautiful bakery and bistro, awash with sunlight and polished woods, filled with men and women in expensive clothes, serious and focused. Voices resonated on low notes, rising and falling. A business crowd. He felt a little out of place in his tweed jacket. Were people looking at him? He reached up and touched the knot of his tie to be sure it was in place.

She undid the buttons on her coat and unwound the green cashmere muffler that caught the color of her eyes. Her cheeks were rosy from the cold, giving her a cheerful appearance. Far too cheerful, as far as he was concerned.

"How do you like Payard?" Mimi asked, sitting down in the chair he was holding out for her. She adjusted herself at the table and shook out her short gray hair with a graceful gesture. It caught the admiring sideward glance of an older, well-dressed man at a neighboring table. The woman sitting with him tapped him impatiently on the arm.

"I love it," Jonathan said. "It's like being back in Paris."

"Wait until you taste the croissants and the coffee. Daniel opened it with Francoise a few years ago."

He looked her in the eye. "Okay, Mimi. I'll bite. Daniel who?"

A waiter came towards them, navigating the narrow spaces between the tables. "Good morning, Mrs. Aaron. It's nice to see you again. Would you like your usual?" A smile and nod. "And for you, sir?"

Mimi resumed from where she'd left off as the waiter wove his way away. "Jonathan! I thought you were a foodie. Daniel who, for goodness sake." Her eyes crinkled into a smile.

"Nope. I'm not a foodie. More of a wino." That's what got me into this mess, he reflected.

"Daniel Boulud, of course. If you've not been to Restaurant Daniel, I must take you. The food is exquisite."

"I look forward to it."

Over coffee, which was every bit as rich and aromatic as Mimi had promised, Jonathan turned to the business at hand. Mimi was taking this meeting with Lieutenant Julian Wayne far too lightly. He knew Wayne from the Fernaud matter. Wayne was a bulldog. An ill-tempered one at that.

"Exactly what did the police say to you when they called?"

"Nothing at all, really. The young man was very polite. He just asked me to come down to the precinct for a meeting with Lieutenant Wayne. He said they just had some follow-up questions. I asked if there was a problem and he said no, it was just routine."

"Mimi, as I told you, there's nothing like routine questions from the police where a death is involved."

"Of course. But if I can help them, I want to. I'm not comfortable about what happened to poor Arthur. If they can find out anything, I'm all for it." She tried her coffee. "Isn't this just excellent?"

They made their way to the nondescript precinct building in the nondescript neighborhood, picking their way carefully along the icy streets. A way Jonathan remembered surprisingly well from his visit four years ago. The little office with the green peeling walls looked the same, down to the half-cup of cold coffee sprinkled with cigarette ash sitting on Lt. Julian Wayne's desk. Only this time the surface of his desk looked like a pharmacy of cold remedies. Wayne looked as disheveled as his office.

The young man who showed them in sat down in a straight-backed chair behind them and opened a stenographer's pad on his knee. Wayne sneezed into a kleenex and tossed it into the wastebasket. He looked up at Jonathan with rheumy brown eyes.

"What are you doin' here?" The emphasis was on "you."

"Good morning, Lieutenant. I'm Jonathan Franklin. We met four years ago."

Mimi raised her head and gave Jonathan an inquiring look. Why hadn't he mentioned he knew Wayne?

"Yeah, I remember. You got it all wrong last time." He gave a halfhearted snort, hampered by his stuffed nose. "That don't answer my question. What are you doin' here?"

"Well, Mrs. Aaron is a friend of mine. She asked me

to come down with her." A police siren screamed outside, its wail piercing the room.

"Are you actin' as her lawyer?"

"Not unless I have to in order to stay." He accompanied the statement with a smile.

"Uh-huh," Wayne concluded, having been through this routine before. He turned towards Mimi. She shifted in her hard chair to a more comfortable position. Her graceful hands were gathered in her lap. "How can I help you, Lieutenant?"

"Mrs. Aaron, there're a few more things we need to get cleared up. I got some questions about this death that don't make a lot of sense to me. Why don't you tell me again about this dog. You said he caused DeRuk's death."

"Yes. Arthur loved the dog. When he was kidnapped I think Arthur snapped."

"How do you mean he was kidnapped?" Wayne looked over Jonathan's shoulder at the man sitting in the back of the room. The young man started scratching furiously at his steno pad.

"Arthur told me there was a ransom demand, a phone call."

"When?"

"It was right around the first of October, as I remember. Just after the beginning of the month."

"Uh-huh. So what happened?"

"Nothing. That was the problem. There was no other call. Arthur didn't know where to deliver the money. He wanted to pay. It drove him mad, the waiting. That's when he had the relapse."

"By this relapse you mean that's when he started shootin' up again, right?"

"Well, that's not precisely how I'd put it, Lieutenant, but yes."

"Tell me again what your relationship was with this guy."

"Well, I'm his executor." Her smile died on her lips.

"No, I mean before he died." That evasion again. Not this time.

"We were close friends." Mimi's mouth firmed. This wasn't where she wanted to go.

"Yeah, that's what you said last time. I wanna know how close?"

"And I told you before, Lieutenant, that's none of your business."

"I think it is."

Jonathan's ears pricked up.

Mimi was silent for a moment. When she responded her words were carefully chosen.

"Arthur and I spent some time together, but nothing came of it."

"Guy's a little young for you, ain't he?"

Mimi flushed.

"I hardly think that's necessary, Lieutenant," Jonathan said.

Wayne ignored him. "Far as we can tell, this guy DeRuk ran around with a lotta women."

"That was part of the problem, Lieutenant. But our relationship never got that serious."

"Uh huh. So no jealousy. No bad feelin's?"

Jonathan interrupted again. "What's this all about, Lieutenant? I understood this death was an accident. An overdose?"

"Well now, Franklin," Wayne responded, turning his cold gaze on him, "that's what we don't know." He wiped his nose, staring at Jonathan. "Perhaps you can tell me. You're real good at this kind of thing, as I recall."

The silent young man sitting behind Jonathan smothered a laugh. It drew him a frown from Wayne. He turned back to Mimi, not waiting for an answer.

"So?"

"Of course not. Arthur and I were friends." To Jonathan's ear she sounded defensive. "That's why he named me as the executor of his estate."

Wayne made a note this time. Mimi shifted in her chair.

"So you were just buddies. Real nice like. No problems."

"No, none." There it was again. That strained tone. What was going on?

"Then maybe you can tell me why you sued him for fraud a few months ago."

Jonathan sat up straight and turned to Mimi. He put his hand on her arm. "I don't want you to answer that question. I don't like the way this is going. You need a lawyer. Now!"

"Nonsense," Mimi responded, shrugging him away with a shake of her head that made her gray hair shiver. "I haven't done anything. There's a perfectly reasonable explanation." She turned back to Wayne.

"Arthur could be something of a scoundrel if you let him get away with it. Charming, but a scoundrel. I wasn't about to let him." She had the same air of determination that Jonathan had noticed when he first met her.

Wayne waited.

"I loaned him some money. Not much, but that wasn't the point."

Wayne sniffed back some mucus. He shuffled some papers on his desk and slipped on his reading glasses.

"You loaned him two hundred and fifty thousand dollars. Isn't that right?" He tapped the pages in front of him with a stubby finger.

"Yes. As I said, not a lot of money. But he kept putting off repaying me. He made a promise. Then he'd make an excuse. Usually a good one. But I have a rule. The first excuse, accepted. The second, maybe. Three and that's it. So I called my lawyer and sued him." She sat stiffly, her hands tightly folded in her lap. There it was, just like that.

"You sued him for fraud?" Wayne asked.

Jonathan could hear a pencil scratching behind him. He had forgotten about the young man back there.

"Arthur was like a mule. You had to hit him over the head with a two-by-four to get his attention." She chuckled to herself, and her gray-green eyes grew warmer. She raised a finger to her lips. The hand with the diamond ring. "When we served him, he telephoned me. He was screaming and shouting. He called me all kinds of names. But he always respected a certain ruthlessness. So after a few days, he called and apologized." A thumb moved over her ring as she turned into her memories.

"Did you get your money back?" Wayne said abruptly.

"Some of it. He told Warren Hovington to pay me. I was getting it by dribs and drabs."

"How much did you get back?

"I don't really remember. Perhaps $50,000."

"And this Arthur DeRuk was just a buddy, huh?" Wayne took off his reading glasses and threw them on the desk. "This Hovington was his dealer, right?"

"Oh, much more than his art dealer, Lieutenant. He took care of all of Arthur's affairs." Mimi relaxed as the conversation turned away from her relationship with Arthur DeRuk. "He managed his money, and really, he managed Arthur's life. Warren Hovington was like Arthur's mother hen, and Arthur could drive him up the wall. He knew how to push his buttons. I could swear that he did it on purpose sometimes."

Wayne sneezed and blew his nose. He waved a germ-laden hand at Mimi. "Sorry. Go on."

"Arthur was always putting things off, you see. He never worked consistently. He got distracted. I was there once when they got into it over a show that was coming up. In any case, Warren was instructed to pay me what Arthur owed."

"So you and this DeRuk guy made it up?"

"That's correct, Lieutenant. I even gave him Rufus as a 'kiss and make up' present."

"Who's this Rufus?"

"Why, Lieutenant, he's the pug that Arthur loved so much. I thought you knew."

Chapter fourteen

Mimi and Jonathan had escaped to a coffee shop around the corner from Wayne's office. Mimi's green muffler was lying carelessly at her side in the red naugahyde booth. The shop was nearly deserted at 11 a.m. The sky had darkened with the threat of snow. It cast an uneasy light into the narrow space.

He leaned forward, nearly upsetting his coffee cup. "You gave DeRuk the dog?" He must have spoken more loudly than he intended. The waitress behind the counter gave him a questioning look. He pushed his wire-rimmed glasses up on his nose and lowered his voice.

"Yes, I thought I told you," Mimi said. "Simon gave me Rufus. It was a sweet, misguided thought. But I didn't want a dog." Her eyes lifted to meet his. "You know how they tie you down. At this point in my life I want to get up and leave when I get the inspiration. Arthur had just apologized. He was very sweet about it. So I gave him Rufus as a gift."

"Oh, great." One more connection to DeRuk's death.

Mimi ignored him. "You should have seen Arthur down on the floor playing with him." She closed her eyes and seemed to catch the picture in her mind. "He had such a beautiful tush," she sighed.

"Who, DeRuk?"

"No. Of course not. Rufus. He was a gorgeous little pug, pure brown, with a black face like an angel. A very ugly angel perhaps," she backtracked. "A face so ugly it was beautiful," she finally concluded. "Anyway, Arthur treated Rufus like his child, and Rufus adored it. He loved the attention. I'd never seen Arthur act that way. So open. He took Rufus with him everywhere. I think he actually loved him. I guess you never know."

The waitress wandered over. "You want some more coffee?" she asked, brandishing the pot. They both shook their heads and she wandered back to the counter. Jonathan turned back to Mimi.

"Don't you see a problem here? Didn't you see the look on Wayne's face? You had access. Christ, you not only had opportunity, you were there. You had motive. He thinks you were crazy jealous about DeRuk's philandering. I don't think he believes a word you said. And you even stood to benefit from Arthur DeRuk's death."

Her eyes cut at him across the table. "Of course I didn't."

"Oh, yes you did." He wasn't going to back off. This was too important. She had to understand. "The executor of a valuable estate will make a lot of money."

"I don't need money."

"I know that, but Wayne doesn't. Some people with lots of money never get enough. And the lawsuit looks awful. For fraud yet. Why didn't you ever mention it?"

"It wasn't important. I never intended to proceed

with it. I just needed to let Arthur know I couldn't be ignored."

"Mimi, come on. He took you for two hundred and fifty thousand dollars and it slipped your mind?"

"Jonathan, don't take that tone with me." Anger flared in her eyes, turning them gray. "Do you have any idea how much I got in the divorce? Two hundred and fifty thousand dollars is less than two weeks' earnings on my capital. It simply wasn't important. But I didn't like the way Arthur wheedled it out of me with a cock-and-bull story about a show and a short-term cash flow problem and then ignored my telephone calls."

"Mimi, Wayne is going to go nuts." Jonathan took off his glasses, a lawyer's move he seldom used. "Look. You just don't get it. For a smart lady you can be incredibly frustrating." He signaled the waitress to refill his coffee.

"I thought you didn't want any," the waitress said, pouring the coffee and slapping a check down on the table.

Jonathan started again. "You're really not taking this seriously. We need to find out a lot more about your Arthur DeRuk. You need to introduce me to some of the people who were around him." His voice rose a note. "If you're not going to take this seriously, I am."

"Jonathan, you really worry too much." She gave a little chuckle. Her eyes crinkled. She raised her cup to her lips, made a face and put it down. "But I do need to talk to you about the estate. I have a problem."

"Oh? Now what."

"There's no money, and don't get snippy. Put your glasses back on. It just seems like there should be money. Several of Arthur's pieces were sold at auction a few weeks ago. Warren Hovington handled it. The pictures brought record prices."

"That's good. There shouldn't be a problem then."

"But there is. When I spoke to Warren he said there had been issues and that he had had to refund the purchase price on three of the four purchases."

"Do you think Hovington is stealing from the estate?"

"Oh! Goodness, no. The pieces are all there. Warren was Arthur's dealer forever. Arthur even made him his art executor. It just seems strange to me, that's all. I don't understand. Would you mind seeing Warren?"

"No. I wanted to meet him anyway."

"Good. He's giving an artist's reception at his gallery for the opening of a show by Essame Quinn, a very promising young artist." She reached forward and placed her hand on top of his. "Take me."

Chapter fifteen

"Mimi, dear. It's Cynthia Edwards. How are you?"

Mimi immediately regretted her decision. She had been on her way out when the phone rang. The morning sun had finally emerged. Ice sparkled on The Pond. Lemon yellow sunlight flooded the living room. She undid her jacket button by button and sat down in one of the pale blue armchairs. Cynthia's voice expressed concern. Too much concern.

"I'm fine. It's a beautiful day. Why are you asking?" Cynthia was her friend, but she had always been a bit of a busybody.

"I'm sure it's nothing. Nothing at all. I got a visit from the police. An Inspector Tritter."

Mimi felt a tightening in her stomach. Suddenly she didn't feel in control. "Oh, what did he want?" She didn't like the idea of people poking around in her comfortable life. What was going on? Wasn't Tritter the young man she'd met who was helping that annoying policeman?

"He asked me questions about you and Arthur."

She gripped the phone tighter. Her knuckles whitened. "Why was he asking questions?" It was a struggle to sound disinterested.

"He wouldn't tell me. I did ask him."

I'll bet, Mimi said to herself. Aloud she just said, "Oh?"

Maria came out of the kitchen. She seemed surprised to see Mimi still there. Mimi put her hand over the receiver. "Maria. Could you bring me a glass of water with some ice, please?"

"Certainly, Misses."

"I apologize, Cynthia," she said, uncovering the phone. "Please go on. This policeman was asking you some questions about me?"

"Yes. I thought they were rather personal questions. He wanted to know if you and Arthur lived together." There was a gleeful ingredient to her concern. "How you got along, whether you were jealous. I thought it all was rather strange."

Maria returned with the glass of ice water and handed it to Mimi. Mimi took a sip.

"What did you tell him?"

"Well dear, he *was* a policeman." Cynthia sounded flustered, as if she didn't expect the question. "I told him I didn't know very much. How you had talked about being engaged. And how upset you were with Arthur when you found out he was seeing someone else. That awful woman. I think that's when you said you were going to sue him for the money he stole."

Good lord, had she told Cynthia that? Was she getting stupid in her old age? "Did you say that to the police, Cynthia?"

"Oh, no, no. Of course not. I wouldn't do anything

to cause you a problem."

Mimi wondered. There had always been a certain bit of tension between them. And in her experience, Cynthia wasn't altogether forthright on occasion.

"Exactly what did you say?" She took another sip of water.

"Well, he kept asking me questions. I avoided them as best I could, of course. But he was a very pushy young man. I don't think I told him anything that would concern you."

Mimi didn't like the sense she was getting from Cynthia. "I..." She had a catch in her throat. She reached for the water glass and sipped again. "Sorry. I do appreciate your letting me know. I really don't have any idea what inspired this. I certainly intend to find out."

"Do let me know if I can do anything." Cynthia sounded almost cheery.

"Of course," said Mimi, hanging up the telephone, certain that Cynthia Edwards had done enough already. As she sat with her hand on the receiver, thinking, the phone rang again.

"Yes?"

"Mrs. Aaron. This is Walter. The doorman."

"Of course, Walter. What is it?"

"I think there's something you should know."

Her next call was to Jonathan.

"Hello." He sounded groggy.

"Oh dear, Jonathan. It's Mimi. I hope I didn't wake you."

"I was just getting up." He still sounded half-asleep. "I had a late night. What's up?"

"The police seem to be contacting my friends as well

as the staff here in the building. People have been looking at me strangely in the elevators, now that I think of it. My God."

"Hold on for just a second," he said. He groped for his glasses among the books on the nightstand. He knocked them onto the floor and went down on his knees, patting the ground to find them. Now he was wide awake. Mimi sounded rattled. Hadn't she expected this? He had tried to warn her.

"Mimi, keep calm. They're just trying to tie up loose ends. Why are you worried? You must have told me a dozen times there's nothing to bother about." He was trying to get out of his pajamas while juggling the phone.

"It's embarrassing."

"Well, yes, I admit that. But your friends will get over it. Besides," he said, "it'll make you more intriguing." He wanted her to laugh.

"That's not why I'm embarrassed," she said awkwardly.

He paused, one foot in the air. "Oh?"

"Perhaps you should come over."

"Why?" He put his foot down.

"I haven't been entirely honest with you."

Chapter sixteen

"So?" Jonathan said. His tweed jacket lay beside him. He had tugged down his tie.

The early promise of good weather had blossomed into a beautiful winter day, again flooding Mimi's apartment with sunlight. The masses of flowers lent the large living room a gay feeling. His thoughts didn't catch the mood.

He sat across from her on the long, light-yellow couch. Two untouched cups of coffee grew cold. The smell of the spring flowers perfumed the air.

"I'm upset," Mimi said. She couldn't keep her eyes on his. Her delicate hands kept worrying the arms of her pale blue chair.

"I got that, Mimi. You're going to wear out the fabric on that chair. What I don't understand yet is why."

She raised her head and met his hazel eyes for the first time.

"Jonathan, I haven't been entirely forthright with

you." She shifted her body and her eyes held his now. "I'm afraid I could be in trouble."

"What are you trying to say?" He reached out and touched her arm. "Did you have anything to do with Arthur DeRuk's death?"

Her hand flew to her mouth. "Oh, goodness. No. Of course not."

"Then what's the trouble?"

Her eyes glistened with a hint of tears. "I just don't know how to explain it." She looked towards the photograph of Arthur DeRuk on the side table. She touched the edge of the frame. "You see, Arthur was more important to me than I actually told you."

"How?" His question was clipped. Unkind, he realized. In a business deal, he was in trouble if his client didn't level with him. He wouldn't know which way to turn in the negotiations. This was a lot worse.

"We were actually talking about—" she lowered her head and almost mumbled, "getting engaged."

"You're kidding!"

She quickly looked up at him with a piercing expression, her jaw set.

"Sorry," he said. "You just surprised me. From everything I know about this guy, he didn't seem like your type."

"That's not everything," she went on. "You might as well know it all."

"Oh God, Mimi."

"Now listen. Listen to me. When I found out Arthur was cheating on me, I was as angry as I've ever been. We had words. That's when I had my lawyer sue him. I wanted to strike out. To hurt him." Her gray hair gave a sharp shake and her mouth hardened. "He hurt me, damn it." A tear touched her cheek, crystal in the sunlight.

Jonathan waited a respectful moment. "I wish you'd been a little more forthright with me. Mimi, you must realize what's going on." He disliked being played the fool. "You've done everything you can to turn the police on to a possible murder, and now you're telling me you had a jealous snit-fit with DeRuk."

"Yes."

"I hope you're not going to tell me you discussed it with your friends."

"Well, damn it, Jonathan, who would you talk to! I had to talk to someone. I felt like I was coming out of my skin. Don't be so damn judgmental."

"I'm not being judgmental. But you've dug yourself a hole and I'm trying to figure out how deep it is. Damn it, Mimi. The first rule when you find yourself in a hole is to stop digging."

"I know." She let her head fall. The crestfallen gesture touched him, and he reached over and put his hand on her arm.

"Why'd you do it?"

"What?" She looked up.

"Turn the police on."

"I don't really know," she sighed. "I just felt like there was something wrong. I didn't feel right about Arthur killing himself. Even accidentally. He wouldn't do that to me. Things were starting to get straightened out."

"Did you actually have the reconciliation you told the police about?"

"Yes. It was very sweet. And I did give Arthur the pug. He loved Rufus."

"Were you—look Mimi, I don't know how to say this delicately—sleeping with him?"

She didn't meet his eyes.

"Not after we broke up. I didn't trust him anymore. We were just being friends. At least for then."

"Is there anything else I should know?"

Mimi hesitated.

"Come on, Mimi, no more surprises."

She sat for a moment, looking down at her ring catching the light. "I think the police are going to find out I wasn't in my apartment when Arthur died."

He looked puzzled. "What?"

"I'm embarrassed to tell you." She pushed up the sleeves on her green cashmere sweater. Her voice grew sharp. "Damn it. I'm a grown woman. I can do whatever I want to."

"Sure. But you need to tell me. Particularly if you think the police are going to find out. I'm not going to judge you."

"I spent the night with an old friend."

"Male or female?"

Her eyes flashed. "Don't be funny. He's a very old friend. I went to his hotel and stayed with him."

"Okay. Someone must have seen you."

She shook her head. "I went there around nine and took the elevator straight up to his floor. I don't think anyone noticed me. I hope not."

"Who was it?"

"I'd rather not say."

"Why?" He was getting annoyed again. Things were complicated enough without her turning coy.

"He's married. And he's a friend of Simon's too."

"Whether he's married or Simon's friend, or whatever, this is serious. I'd rather have you off the hook and a little embarrassed than the key suspect in a murder case."

"No."

"Mimi. This doesn't make any sense. Why not? And why would you be involved with a married man?"

"I know it doesn't make sense. We weren't really involved. He's truly a friend. Sometimes I just get lonely. He was in town. He called. I like him. He feels comfortable."

She seemed to be straining to justify herself. Perhaps to justify herself to herself.

"He's an Englishman. He and his wife have gone their own way for years. But he won't get divorced. He's charming and accomplished. He was a friend of Simon's and mine when we were married. Look, it just happened."

"He'll still have to back you up if it comes to that. You really do need an alibi."

"No. I won't do it. It would hurt him and it would hurt Simon. I'm not going to let that happen." She rose and walked over to the window and turned back. He caught a hint of her now-familiar perfume as she moved. "Besides, it wouldn't do any good."

"Why not?"

"He had a morning flight. We got up very early." She returned to the armchair and sat down. "It was before five o'clock when I left the hotel."

"No one saw you leave?"

"No, I don't think so."

"Tell me exactly what you did after you left. Maybe there's some other way to verify where you were."

"I didn't feel like going back to my apartment. I wanted to walk. I like the city when it's quiet. I window-shopped for a while. Then I thought about Arthur. I guess I still didn't want to be alone. Maybe I felt a little guilty. It was around eight. I stopped by Wolfe's to get some chicken soup."

"Do you think someone would remember you? Did

anything unusual happen?"

She shook her head. "Maybe, but I don't think so. I left and took the soup up to Arthur's apartment. That's when I found him."

"So no one saw you between five and eight in the morning, except the cashier at Wolfe's?"

"Not that I know of."

"Great," said Jonathan, biting his lip. "Really just perfect."

Chapter seventeen

"So what happened to Elly Warren?" Jonathan whispered.

He had heard the rumors before he left Cambridge. He was sitting at a table under the murals in the Rotunda room of the Hotel Pierre in one of the soft lounge chairs when his cell phone rang. It had prompted a dirty look from the well-dressed woman sitting next to him, so he was whispering.

He had retreated to the Pierre after his meeting with Mimi Aaron. He needed to think. Ben Cohen, the dean of the Harvard Law School, had tracked him down to deliver the news.

"She was tapped to run Metadyne Industries. You know she came to the business school from industry. I don't think she ever got it out of her blood."

He understood that all too well.

"It's a real loss," Cohen continued. "She pumped a lot of life into the place." There was a moment of silence.

"Besides, she gave us some great stock tips," he chuckled. "But I think Kurt West will do a good job as dean. I'm afraid he has some strange ideas though."

"Oh?" said Jonathan, patiently waiting for the reason that Ben Cohen had sought him out during the winter break. It wasn't shaping up to be a good day.

"It's gotten a little political over there since Elly left. They're a bit uneasy with how many of their courses are being taught by our law school people."

"Ben, you know the course I'm teaching on mergers & acquisitions is a joint JD/MBA course."

"I know. But it's under the business school's imprimatur." Cohen paused. "Uh, I think they're looking closely at your course."

"Why? I've had good attendance. I have a waiting list. As far as I can tell, the kids love it. The feedback has been great." Jonathan raised his voice, drawing another dirty look he ignored.

He was starting to feel defensive and a little hostile. He didn't like the way this was going. Ben Cohen was beating around the bush.

"Well—if I had to guess, I'd bet Kurt thinks it should be taught by one of his guys. He wants to reorganize the course."

"Ben, damn it. I've been giving the course for two years now. I've put a hell of a lot of work into it, and we're just hitting our stride. I've got some great ideas for next year. It's just getting interesting now, with the changes in market dynamics since the Internet bubble burst. The kids could really learn something."

"Jonathan, I'm sorry."

"Can I do anything?" Resignation closed in on him.

"I don't think so. Kurt was pretty insistent when he talked to me. To tell you the truth, I don't think he likes lawyers very much."

Jonathan gave a hollow laugh. "Join the club," he said. He realized that he was gripping his cell phone. He relaxed his hand.

"He feels that the course should be more analytically grounded in the conceptual end," Cohen continued. "You know. How do you decide if a company fits? How to analyze the numbers? What are the synergies?"

"We do that with outside people we bring in from Wall Street," Jonathan said. "That's their *raison d'être*. But it's got to be balanced against a hard-nosed business attitude." He pushed his glasses back up on his nose. The woman at the next table was starting to mutter. "The investment bankers have never seen a deal they didn't like. They only get paid at closing. That's why I have them on a panel with guys in charge of development from some of the biggest S&P 500 companies. It's really been working. We've had great discussions."

"I know. This is no reflection on you. But there's nothing I can do. It's Kurt's decision. You can call him if you want to. But I don't think it'll do any good. I'm sorry to be the bearer of bad tidings."

Shit! He snapped his cell phone shut. He was really enjoying that class. Sometimes he thought the politics at school were so damn nasty because the stakes were so small.

He got up and wandered into the lobby, the woman at the next table giving him a stern look as he passed. He looked out at the snowy street and wondered whether he had made the right decision five years ago to leave Whiting & Pierce. Jonathan reached into his pocket and began absently rubbing the little silver snuff-box his father had given him when he went off to college. "A family heirloom," his father had said. "Ben Franklin's. For luck."

He had taken to carrying it after his father died.
Luck. Now it seemed like every piece of his life was
moving. The wrong way.

Chapter eighteen

People parted within the white gallery walls to let the red-coated waiters pass, bearing trays of champagne and wine. Jonathan and Mimi handed their coats and gloves to the young woman at the door before turning to the sound of Warren Hovington's voice rising above the chatter.

"Ah, Mimi, my dear." He took her small hand in both of his. "I'm so pleased we could entice you out on such a cold night for our little reception."

The weather had turned rock cold in the last day. Sleet and ice had made the trek to SoHo a challenge. Mimi had insisted they go, even over Jonathan's heartfelt objections. It was far too cold to venture out.

"Do you know Essame Quinn's work?" Hovington's sweeping gesture took in walls of canvases painted in black and brown lines. Warren Hovington didn't seem to pause. "A wonderful talent. Not readily accessible like Arthur, of course. He believes art should reach down inside and wring out emotions. His art is disturbing, but rewarding if you allow it the attention to let it grow."

What the hell did he just say? Jonathan looked over at Mimi. She was listening with her head cocked to the side, a half smile in her gray-green eyes.

"And who might this be?" Hovington asked in his well-turned voice, looking towards Jonathan.

"Warren, I'd like you to meet Professor Jonathan Franklin of the Harvard Law School. He's an old friend of Simon's and mine."

Hovington delivered his practiced handshake. "A pleasure to meet you, Professor Franklin."

Jonathan looked at the tall, thin man with the hooded blue eyes. So this is Warren Hovington. Nostrils flared in an aquiline nose. He was dressed in a black cashmere turtleneck, his long silver hair tied back into a ponytail.

A heavyset older woman in a black dress came up behind them and put her hand on Hovington's arm. He turned to make room for her.

"Thank you for doing this, Warren. We so appreciate your thoughtfulness. It's rare in our community to find people who care and who are so generous with their resources and their time."

Hovington gave her a modest smile and a small nod. "Deborah, it's a pleasure, really. Your organization does such good work. Animal rescue is so necessary. No thanks are required. I'm happy to do what I can." His smile returned to Mimi. He raised his hand towards her.

"Deborah, may I introduce Mimi Aaron and Professor Jonathan Franklin. Mimi, Jonathan, this is Deborah Kingmore, the chairman of Animal Rescue here in New York."

Wow, he can remember all the names, Jonathan thought.

"Warren," Mimi said, "I didn't know you were involved in animal rescue too. What a worthy cause."

Hovington opened his mouth to respond.

"Oh, yes," the older woman said, cutting him off. "Warren is one of our most important supporters. He's donating ten percent of the proceeds from this reception to us."

"Well, bravo to you, Warren," Mimi said warmly.

Deborah Kingmore glanced around. "Mrs. Aaron, Professor Franklin. It was nice to meet you. I hope to see you again. Please excuse me. I have to circulate. We have so many supporters here."

Hovington seemed a bit embarrassed. He changed the subject quickly. "I really am so glad you could come, Mimi."

"I thought Jonathan would enjoy your exhibit."

"You're most welcome here, Professor Franklin," Hovington said, making hooded eye contact with Jonathan. "Mimi is one of our most valued friends. Come let me introduce you both to the artist. He's right over there," Hovington said, pointing to a short, stocky man of perhaps 45, with thinning dark hair. He was standing alone in a far corner. His full gray beard obscured the front of his tie and jacket. He clutched a glass of red wine, looking uncomfortable.

"Essame," Hovington called out above the clatter, gesturing to Quinn, "I want you to meet someone." Quinn finished the wine in a gulp and started across the room.

"Essame, meet Mimi Aaron and her friend Jonathan Franklin. I've been telling them about your work."

Quinn put down his empty wineglass and shook hands grudgingly. It was hard to tell if he was shy or angry. Jonathan jumped in.

"Mr. Quinn, your work is quite impressive." Particularly impressive since Jonathan didn't know what he was talking about. "Can you tell me your thoughts behind this picture?" he said, pointing to a large painting that appeared to him to be the scrawlings of a deranged small animal that had broken into the paint cupboard.

"No," Quinn snapped. He glared at Jonathan from dark brown eyes, bushy eyebrows twisting. "I never talk about my work. It ruins the expression. I believe understanding art requires thought, not a lecture."

"Ah," said Jonathan.

Hovington shrugged imperceptibly, as if to say "You see how it is and what I have to put up with."

"Is this your first one-man show, Mr. Quinn?" Mimi interjected to ease the awkward silence.

Quinn bristled and stared intently at Hovington. Jonathan noticed that his rough hands were clenched into fists. What a strange man.

"Oh, Essame was an important artist for us a little while ago," Hovington answered for Quinn. "And he just rejoined our gallery. He's been working for several years to prepare this show. If you would, it represents a major turning point in his artistic maturity." He tipped his head, his ponytail canting, as he gave the nearest painting a restrained nod.

Quinn didn't seem mollified. He still stared at Hovington, muscles working at the corners of his jaw.

"Then you knew my friend Arthur DeRuk?" Mimi said, turning towards Quinn.

Quinn said nothing.

Jonathan's gaze was turned inward. He had been thinking about how to approach Hovington. After all, it was the purpose of coming out on this dreadful night. Now Mimi had just delivered him the perfect opening.

"Yes, Mr. Hovington," he cut in, "I'm also interested in Mr. DeRuk's work, and Mrs. Aaron was telling me you're his art executor. I would enjoy sitting down with you and discussing it some day. When you have the time."

It was too much for Quinn. "That son of a bitch," he shouted.

Jonathan jumped. He had no idea who Quinn was shouting at or why. Hovington's face froze. His thin mouth gaped open. People around them stopped talking and stared.

"Now, now, Essame, don't speak ill of the dead," Hovington said, recovering. He put a restraining hand on Quinn's arm.

Quinn wrenched his arm away. "Good riddance to the bastard. I'm glad he's dead," Quinn stalked off, jostling a red-coated waiter. A tray of glasses crashed to the floor.

Hovington turned to Mimi and Jonathan. "I'm so sorry. He and Arthur had a difficult relationship. I'm afraid Essame is not very politic. But that's what makes him a great artist," he said, gesturing vaguely to the paintings. As he spoke he was looking over Mimi's shoulder towards the door.

"Please do excuse me. I must say hello to some new guests. Feel free to look around. If you have any questions, my staff will be happy to help you, or just ask me. Professor Franklin," he added as an afterthought, "please call me. I'd be happy to sit down with you." He moved off toward the new guests, his hand held out, ponytail gleaming.

Jonathan turned to Mimi. "Mr. Quinn doesn't seem to like your Arthur very much, does he?"

"Not very, I'd say."

"I'll call Hovington tomorrow and set up an appointment. I'll see what I can find out. I don't think Quinn is going to be very receptive to chatting with me. Is there anybody else here I should meet?"

"Let's circulate and see," she said, motioning for the waiter coming towards them.

Apparently '80s chic was back. There was a predominance of black outfits on the bustling, chattering crowd. They clutched wineglasses and milled among the pictures in the shimmering gallery space. He felt out of place in his herringbone tweed jacket and tie.

Two glasses of wine and a battery of small talk later, Mimi leaned towards Jonathan. She applied a small pressure to his arm while glancing up towards a lithe, dark-haired Asian woman in her late twenties or early thirties. The woman was dressed in a black silk, loose-fitting top and a long black skirt. Around her neck was a thin red choker collar of some material Jonathan couldn't identify. It matched her eye shadow.

"That's Myacura Ishii. She and Arthur were very close at one time," Mimi said, her words carrying a noticeable strain. She continued before Jonathan could formulate a question. "They had a terrible falling out. You should meet her, but not with me." Jonathan leaned close to Mimi as she whispered. "We never got on. In any case, I'm tired. I think I'll catch a cab and talk to you tomorrow."

"Can I get the cab for you? It's really cold out there. And this isn't the best of neighborhoods."

"Don't be silly. I'm a big girl. Besides, Warren will get me one. I'll be fine." She gave him a gallery peck on the cheek and moved towards the door with a little wave over her shoulder. Jonathan was left to contemplate the woman she had pointed out. Interesting. He made his way over to the painting that Myacura Ishii was pondering.

"Hi," he said. "What do you make of this thing?"

Chapter nineteen

Her deep brown eyes were concentrated on him. He noticed they had yellow flecks in them. She was really quite attractive. Her red silk choker emphasized her long neck. She smelled like spice. They were sitting in a dark paneled corner of the Oak Room at the Plaza Hotel with a spent bottle of '95 Dom Perignon between them. The crowd had thinned and it was quieter now. Almost midnight.

" . . . Rather insular in nature, derived from the Color Field esthetic, but turned on its head," she concluded. She was discussing her view of Essame Quinn's work. They had been talking for hours.

"You really seem to understand this stuff. It's more than I can say."

Intelligent, he noted. And intriguing. He was starting to get turned on. Intelligent women did that to him. Attractive, intelligent women. He reached to put his hand on her arm, then thought better of it and drew back his hand.

She noticed his gesture and smiled. "I've been interested in art for years. I guess it's one of the reasons I got involved with Arthur DeRuk."

"Why did you break up?" It was a question that he had been waiting to ask.

"Arthur was a lot of fun. But kind of a bastard," she said. Her long black hair moved sinuously as she shook her head. It was the continuation of a conversation they had been having off and on since Jonathan had asked her to have a drink with him and they had left the gallery. "And he had a thing for older women. Who needed it?" Her hand made an involuntary fist on the table. She took a sip of champagne. "He was a mean drunk and selfish deep down. He hurt people. I couldn't put up with him anymore." She sank back in her chair and let her hand fall in her lap. Jonathan noticed her long red fingernails.

"The man had no taste," said Jonathan, feeling lightheaded and charming.

It was a game he played with pretty women. Was he attractive? Would they sleep with him? It was a kind of flaw inside him somewhere. He had thought about it. Maybe it was a need for his mother's approval. Whatever! But it was trouble. If he was appealing in a way he hardly understood, and if a woman responded, it was even harder to disappoint her. Damn near impossible in fact. At least for him.

"Do you like teaching law?" she said, changing the subject. She leaned forward. He caught a glimpse of the dusky swelling of her breasts.

"It's okay. I love the law school. I can live in the country and have all the stimulation Harvard can provide. And I really like the kids. They're always coming up with something new." He waved away the waiter coming towards their table. "But sometimes the politics gets to me. Think of it as a vat of crabs with their big pincers opening and closing, crawling and scraping over each other."

It occurred to him in a hazy way that he was beginning to sound bitter. He'd have to think about that.

"I love the way you dress," she said, interrupting his thoughts. She had a teasing smile on her face. "A tweed jacket is so unusual around the gallery scene."

"Thank you. I think." Her smile broadened. He pushed his wire-rimmed glasses back up on his nose. "And how about you? What do you do?"

"Oh, I work at *Vogue*. I'm an assistant arts editor. I sculpt as well. I wanted to be an artist, but it just wouldn't keep body and soul together. That's how I met Arthur. Why don't you come up and take a look when you drop me off?"

"Love to," he said. He knew as he said it that it was a mistake.

An hour later he was sitting on the couch in her small flat in TriBeca, another glass of wine in his hand. He had mixed emotions. On the one hand, he was having a pretty good time. He hadn't been in a strange woman's apartment in almost four years. It was titillating. On the other hand, he knew he was in trouble. He knew he was in trouble because he had been there before.

She leaned across the small couch, reached up and turned his head to hers. Her black hair brushed against the side of his face. She kissed him. His hand, acting on its own, went under her black silk top to her small naked breast. The nipple hardened against his fingers. She increased the pressure of her kiss and made a low sound in her throat. Her hand brushed against the front of his trousers.

* * *

He woke up about three in the morning in a sense of panic. Myacura Ishii was sleeping beside him, her naked body curved against his. He scuttled away carefully.

"Oh, shit," he said, rolling softly out of bed. He groped for his glasses. "What have I gotten myself into now?"

She stirred in her sleep and he froze on the edge of the bed. When her breathing became regular again he dropped to his hands and knees, patting the floor in the dark room, his naked ass in the air, trying to remember where he'd shed his clothes. This was all incredibly stupid.

Every sound was exaggerated. Every time Myacura Ishii stirred, he held his breath. It seemed like a long time. Damn it, where's that other sock? Finally he found everything. He tiptoed barefoot and naked towards the dim moonlight of the living room.

He sat there with the lights out and put on his clothes as quietly as he could. Then he crossed to the door in small steps, holding his shoes in his hands, trying not to trip over anything in the shadows. He thought about leaving a note, but that didn't seem like such a good idea.

He closed the door behind him, holding the edge so it wouldn't slam, then he sat down on the steps to put on his shoes. The street was silent at three-fifteen in the morning. He was sweating and the cold hit him like a physical blow. He was shivering when he finally found a cab. Only part of his shivering was from the weather. It was four o'clock when he let himself into Nicole's apartment.

"Thank God she's in London," he thought. He shook his head as he slipped into the shower. He needed to wash off the smell of Myacura Ishii.

"Asshole," he said aloud. A vague thought flitted through his mind. He had better get some help with the investigation of Arthur DeRuk. He sure wasn't doing too well on his own.

He lay awake staring at the ceiling, considering the mess he was in. He rearranged the pillow. Then he turned over on his right side, but no matter what position he was in, his mind still struggled.

The early light disturbed her sleep. Ishii awoke slowly and stretched out her arm. Her red lips went slack when her searching hand found the empty bed. She threw back the covers and called out. Silence.

She swore aloud. She wasn't going to let this happen to her. Damn it! Her fist hit the covers again and again and again.

Chapter twenty

"Frankee, its Jonathan Franklin. It's been a long time."

It was twenty past eleven in the morning. He had gotten up a few minutes earlier to make the call. He was in his pajamas, nursing a cup of coffee, slumped in one of the wooden chairs at the breakfast table. His head hurt.

Frankee Perone was the head of Perone, Brill & Co., one of the most respected investigatory agencies in the country. She had built a far-reaching organization filled with ex-CIA, FBI and Interpol professionals to serve her diverse clientele. Over the years, she had undertaken sensitive matters for Jonathan and his clients, including one involving Nicole DeSant four years ago. But Frankee was an acquired taste.

"Oh, my goodness," she said into the phone with a deliberate primness. Turning away, she shouted, "Katie bar the door, women into the back room. It's that maniac Jonathan Franklin on the phone." Then she turned back to the receiver. "Why, Professor Franklin. I'm fine. How can I be of help?"

"Come off it, Frankee." He stifled a yawn. "This is business. I need you." He paused, remembering the last time he had used Frankee Perone and the favors he had called in with her. "And I'm going to pay," he said quickly. "When can I see you?"

"You just said the magic words. How soon can you be here?"

"An hour."

"See you then. Make sure you bring your checkbook." A moment's silence. "Oh, and be sure to come to the new offices."

The agency had moved to more "corporate" headquarters since he was last there. Sleek glass and polished wood, they reflected the aura of Perone, Brill's major clients. He was led down a long hall to a large corner office, spartan but somehow luxurious. Frankee rose from behind her richly-grained cherry-wood-and-steel desk and extended her hand, a mischievous smile on her lips. Still squarely built, muscular, now in her late 50's, she hadn't gained an ounce. Her gray hair was cut into a crew. On her it still looked feminine. Maybe it was the blue eyes. But she looked every bit the former FBI agent she had been.

"I see you're still in uniform," she said, nodding towards his tweed jacket.

He took her hand. "You do have a good memory, Frankee. Yes, still the college professor, dropping around with my checkbook in hand to pass the time of day." He patted his jacket on the side where he kept his wallet. "All kidding aside, Mimi Aaron's got a problem, and I need some answers."

She motioned him to the couch. She took one of the chairs opposite. "Simon's wife?"

"Ex."

"Okay, what do you need?" Her tone now was all business. Simon Aaron had been an important client for Perone, Brill and would be again. Not someone to be ignored. "You want some coffee?"

He shook his head. "About a month or so ago, an artist named Arthur DeRuk died. It looked like an over-dose. It may have been an accident. Maybe not." He was interrupted by the ring of his cell phone. He fished it out of his pocket and looked at the display. He hit the "end" button to divert the call. She waited patiently for him to look up.

"So?"

"I need to know as much as I can about DeRuk and the people around him. Warren Hovington was his art dealer and he's now the art executor of his estate. There's a guy called Essame Quinn, another artist who apparently didn't think much of DeRuk. And a woman—" Jonathan paused as his mind flashed back, "named Myacura Ishii, a former girlfriend. If anyone else turns up, I want background on them too."

She pulled a pad out of a drawer in the coffee table. "Give me the spelling on those names. Addresses too and anything else you know."

He reached into his pocket for the notes he had hastily prepared before leaving the apartment and handed them to her.

"Okay. What's your interest?"

"Mimi found the body. Her fingerprints were all over. I think the police are suspicious. They're making strange inquiries. I want to know what's going on."

"Who's handling it?"

"Lieutenant Julian Wayne. Heard of him?"

She made a note on her pad. "Yeah, a real hard-ass of a cop, but pretty good. Homicide. If he's got his teeth into it, he won't let go. How soon?"

"As quickly as possible."

Frankee looked directly into his hazel eyes and gave him a big smile. "Well, hot shot, get out your checkbook. You know the drill. My retainer's now $35,000. Where are you staying?"

"I'm at Nicole's," he said while writing the check. "But the best way to reach me is on my cell phone." He gave her the number again.

"How are you and Nicole doing?"

"Just swell," he said, feeling his stomach tighten as he tore out the check. He handed it across to her. He made a note to get himself reimbursed by Simon.

"I'll be in touch," Frankee said as she placed the check like a bookmark between the pages of her writing pad. "Real soon."

Chapter twenty-one

Simon Aaron's Gulfstream G-5 thumped down and reversed thrust on its engines. Jonathan felt the jolt and the pull against his seat belt. It was good to be reconnected to the earth. Slowing, the G-5 turned off the runway and taxied towards the Signature Aviation FBO at the Santa Barbara airport. The co-pilot stepped into the cabin.

"We're here right on time, Professor Franklin. Hope you enjoyed the flight. You have great weather for your stay."

The plane came to a stop. The co-pilot swung open the hatch and pressed the switch to lower the boarding stairs. "We'll be here when you're ready to go back to New York. Give us a few hours' notice."

Jonathan stepped out into a sun-saturated December day with a soft breeze off the ocean caressing his face. He slipped off his tweed jacket, folded it over his arm and pulled down his tie. He rolled up his sleeves as he descended the stairs.

A deeply tanned older man with salt and pepper hair, wearing a cowboy hat and a blue denim shirt over clean blue jeans, strode over to the bottom of the stairs and held out his hand. His eyes matched his denim shirt, and he had the strong hands of a man who used them to make a living. His crinkly smile was infectious.

"Dastel Zager. Call me Day. Simon phoned and said you were comin' out. Thought I'd drive down here and meet you. We can chat on the way back."

"Wow, what a gorgeous day. It was 27 degrees in New York when I left. Is it always like this?"

"Oh, just another average day in paradise," Zager said. "Car's over there." He pointed towards a dark green Range Rover parked by the side of a building. "You need anything before we leave? It'll be 'bout an hour's drive."

Day Zager was nothing like what Jonathan had expected. He was neither a farmer nor the slick marketer of luxury wines. Even dressed in blue jeans, he seemed more like a sophisticated businessman on a long slow holiday that he was thoroughly enjoying.

The Range Rover made its way up into the mountains, opening a sweeping view overlooking Santa Barbara with the deep blue of the Pacific Ocean lapping up against the coast. The winding highway flowed past brown hillsides touched with green. Rock faces showed their teeth where the hills had been scraped aside for the road. They had been driving for about thirty minutes.

"You make some magnificent wines," Jonathan said, breaking the silence. "Some of the best Pinot Noir I've ever tasted."

"Well, we sure try. We've had some success with our

Pinot these last few years. We've got some good stuff in the barrels too. I'd like you to taste it. Our first Syrah'll be bottled and released next year. I think it's terrific."

"How long have you owned the winery, Day?"

"Oh, let's see," Zager paused, counting on his fingers. "About twelve years now, I guess. We've been buying up more land and planting vines in the last few years. I want to only use our own grapes real soon. Control the quality and the yield better that way. And I'd like to do single vineyard wines."

"How'd you get into the wine business? Family?"

"Not hardly," Zager laughed. "My dad was a salesman. Machine tools. I grew up in Indiana before I went East. Not many wineries in Indiana."

"No, not as I recall." Jonathan smiled. This was a nice guy. Maybe it came from working the land.

"I'm a recovering doctor."

"Really."

"What with Medicare and HMO's and everything, I was tending to my paperwork more than my patients. It's kind of like that joke about the plumber."

"Tell me."

"Well, the plumber comes over to a doctor's house and works for half an hour and gives the doctor a bill for two hundred dollars." Zager concentrated on the twisting two-lane road, turning towards Jonathan occasionally as he spoke. His blue eyes were smiling. "The doctor gets all huffy and says 'I'm a doctor and I went to school for eight years. Then I interned and after that I did my residency. It took me three more years to become a specialist. Why this is more than I charge.' The plumber says, 'Well, yeah, it's more than I charged too when I was a doctor.' Seemed to me that there were better things to do with my time when I got near on to 50. I'd saved a bit of money."

"Boy, have I been there."

"I loved drinking wines," Zager said. "Collected loads of it like a lot of doctors. I decided to see how to make it. Took a slew of classes at U.C. Davis up near Sacramento. Discovered I liked it so much I up and quit, and here I am."

They were sweeping by a big lake on their right. "That's Lake Cachuma," Day said, pointing with his chin. "Holds most of the water we use hereabouts. Pretty low right now. Haven't had a lot of rain."

Jonathan went quiet for a moment, taking in the view of the lake, cupped in the brown hands of the surrounding hills. Then he looked over at Zager. "Do you make the wines?" he asked.

"Nope. Not good enough. Oversee the vineyards and generally run the business. I have a great young winemaker. Been with me now for about a year."

"Why only a year?"

"We had some problems with my last guy. Got his thumb stuck in the barrel."

"Ouch, that must have hurt."

"A metaphor. He was scamming us."

"Does that kind of thing happen here too?" Jonathan squirmed in his seat to find a comfortable position. They had been driving for over an hour.

"Not too often. But he got us pretty good. Pretty smart too."

"What happened?"

"He used the old bartender's trick. Worked with him every day. Never spotted it. Wouldn't have either if one of our salesmen hadn't fussed. Seems like he went to a restaurant for dinner and saw our wines on the menu. Complained we screwed him out of his commission."

"What's the bartender's trick?" Jonathan asked. For a

small moment Lieutenant Wayne, Mimi, Myacura Ishii
and the very dead Arthur DeRuk were far away.

Chapter twenty-two

Zager's face took on interesting shadows in the slanting light as he drove on past the lake and entered the low rolling hills of the Santa Ynez Valley.

"Never heard of the bartender's trick, huh? Well, it's cute."

Jonathan turned in his seat towards Zager and adjusted the seat belt to a more comfortable position.

"You know how if you run a bar, the bartender'll steal you blind. So most bars do weekly audits of the bottles and inventory. Even mark the level of the open bottles to keep the bartenders from pouring free drinks for the tips. Bartender can water the booze, but chances are the customers will start to complain."

"Sounds like a smart way to do business."

"Yeah, but one day the bartender figures it out. He doesn't steal your booze. He steals your customers."

"I don't understand."

Zager turned his head towards Jonathan to catch his

eye and quickly turned back to the road. "He brings in his own bottles and pours from his stock, not yours. Your receipts drop off and you can never figure out why unless you sit in the bar all day and watch him."

"But doesn't he have to pay for the liquor?"

"Sure, but it's a high profit business. And the guy's got no overhead."

"You're right. Real smart, but what did your ex-wine-maker do?"

"He brought in three of his own barrels."

"You're kidding."

"No, it's not that hard. When I show you the winery, you'll see. We have hundreds of barrels and they're every-where. Anyway, he filled them with our juice and treated them just like all the others. He probably bottled the wine at night on our line. But he got greedy and used our labels. We get a super premium price."

"What did he steal?"

"Well, it's a little hard to say, you know? A barrel is 60 gallons. That's about 300 bottles of wine. We get $22 and change a bottle, wholesale, and he had 3 barrels. So that's around $20,000 a year. Depends on how long he did it. But with things the way they are with the winery, we could've used the money."

"Simon said you had problems. I've looked over the financial statements. Things don't look so good."

Zager's brow furrowed and his open blue eyes clouded. He looked back at Jonathan again. "Well, that's true in one sense and maybe not so true in another." He gestured to his left.

"Look, we're coming up on the start of our vine-yards now. The winery is about half a mile on. Let's wait till I show you how we operate and maybe give you some idea of how the business works, and then we can talk about it over dinner."

* * *

They drove down a long driveway bordered on both sides by rows of naked grapevines. They came over a rise in the gently rolling hills to a large Spanish-style house with a big barn to one side. Zager pulled the Range Rover in beside the barn. "Come on," Day Zager said, slipping out of the car and motioning for Jonathan to follow. "Let me show you around." He made a sweeping gesture with his big hand as he walked towards the barn. "It's pretty quiet now that harvest's over. You should see it around here then."

The inside of the barn had been gutted and replaced with a spic-and-span, concrete-and-stainless-steel winery. High stacks of large wooden barrels and a smattering of smaller ones occupied one whole end of the large space. Air conditioning hummed and Jonathan slipped back into his jacket. The heavy, pleasant smell of damp grapiness hung in the dark, cool air.

"We keep it pretty cold in here so the wine won't get stressed as it ages."

"This place is a lot bigger than it looks." And really costly, he thought. "How much wine do you produce?"

"We're pretty small. We release around 25,000 cases a year of Pinot Noir and Chardonnay."

"That sounds like a lot to me." He blew on his cold hands.

"Nah." Zager's blue eyes softened as he looked around the barn. "The big wineries produce hundreds of thousands of cases a year. But we want to really concentrate on very high quality handmade wines."

"Sounds expensive."

"It is."

Jonathan pointed to some big stainless-steel tanks.

"What are those?"

"Those are fermenters. With the Pinot, we pick and cold soak the grapes for four or five days. Then we add special yeast to start the fermentation. We hand punch the grapes several times a day. The total time on the skins is around 20 days. We draw off the free run juice into those new oak barrels. See the empties over there." He pointed towards a corner of the barn.

"Free run?" Jonathan shoved his hands into his pockets. He found the little silver snuffbox warm and comforting to his touch.

"When you're dealing with a quality wine, you only use the juice that runs off from the weight of the grapes without pressing them. We prune our grapes back pretty hard for good concentration. Then we only use the free run juice. If we pressed them we'd get a lot more juice, but the wine would be more tannic and coarser."

He half sat down on the edge of a barrel and faced Jonathan. "This all old hat to you? I don't want to bore you."

"No. It's fascinating. I drink the stuff, but that's all. Please go on." Maybe this winery investment stuff wasn't as bad as he thought.

"Anyway, the wine undergoes an aging process in the new oak, we call it malolactic fermentation, and then after a year it's transferred into French oak barrels. We replace half of those every year. It rests there for another six months, then it's bottled and released. We bottled last week," he said, getting up.

He put his hand on Jonathan's shoulder. "But, unless you want to look around some more, let me show you to your room so you can shower and freshen up. I'll have someone grab your bags. We're having some guests in for a little dinner party at seven. Thought you might enjoy it.

They're in the business too. You also might find it useful."

"Can't wait." But even as he said it, he wondered how Frankee Perone was making out.

Chapter twenty-three

Jonathan's room was large and appointed in earth tones. Wide, deep windows flooded the room with a dusky light. The brightly-striped horse blanket on the bed added a flash of dark green and yellow. He felt a surge of well-being. Thick, rough walls gave the room a cool Spanish feel. A bottle of 2000 Zager Pinot Noir with two wine glasses and a corkscrew had been placed on the table by the bed. Nice touch.

He shed his coat. As he was about to toss it on the king-sized bed, he felt the weight in the side pocket. He fished out his cell phone.

Damn it. Forgot to turn it on. He hadn't heard from Nicole all day. That was unusual. The thought of Nicole brought a smile to his lips, then the anxiety touched him. A child! He felt like he couldn't breathe.

He punched the button and the phone lit up with a beep. "Eight missed calls" flashed on the screen. He sat down on the bed.

He pushed the "listen" button, holding the phone to his ear. Maybe Nicole had had second thoughts. Or worse, maybe not.

"Jonathan, darling," said a voice he didn't recognize. "I enjoyed seeing you so much. Why didn't you leave me a note?" His chest tightened. "Call me." She gave a number that he didn't know. He stood up and strode to one of the large windows. The low brown hills rolled away as far as he could see.

Skip.

"Why haven't you called? I miss you. It's Myacura."

Delete. His hand clenched the phone.

How did she get his telephone number? Did he give her his card?

Listen, skip.

Listen, skip.

"It's been six hours. I won't be treated like this! Damn you." Bang.

Delete. He felt a knot in his stomach.

Listen, skip.

Listen, skip.

She was getting more worked up with each call. It was like some lovesick teenager. Or some emotionally unstable person. Maybe the same thing. It had only been a day, for God's sake.

What the hell kind of person have I gotten myself involved with? He punched up the eighth call. Ishii's tone now was hysterical. Was she high?

"Damn you!" Ishii shouted. "You won't call me back, will you! You think I'm some kind of cheap slut you can pick up in a gallery and fuck and forget. Well, I'm not. You asshole! I know you're seeing someone. I won't let you get away with it!"

Shit. What a time for this. He stared at the horse

blanket, thinking. If she contacted Nicole, he was screwed. She'd never understand. That stopped him. Would she? No. It was more likely she'd disembowel him. If she didn't aim lower.

Sweat was starting to soak through his shirt even though it was a pleasant, comfortable evening. He bit his lower lip.

Maybe he could call her. Ishii, that is.

What would he say?

He thought about that for a moment. "It was all a terrible mistake . . . I was drunk. Sorry." He didn't think it would fly.

He glanced at his watch. He had been standing in the same spot for five minutes. The time for dinner was approaching. He started to undress.

I sure don't see how I'm going to get out of this. Shit. Maybe there's someone who can get Myacura Ishii to be reasonable. Fat chance.

He went into the bathroom and turned the shower on hot. His glasses steamed over in the moist heat. He took them off and threw them onto the gray granite sink top with a clink. He unstrapped his watch and put it on the counter beside his glasses.

Mimi knows her, he remembered suddenly. Could she help? Did he even want to involve her?

He placed a fingertip on the mirror and looked absently at the tiny shiny spot. Then he stepped into the shower and moved his head under the stinging water.

Chapter twenty-four

Warren Hovington was engaged in a delicate act of client management, and he didn't like it. No, he didn't like it at all.

"Essame, the show was wonderful." He lifted a forkful of crab salad to his mouth and chewed it slowly, gauging Quinn's mood. "Your art is spectacular. It was everything I had hoped."

A grunt.

They were sitting in the dining room of the Royalton. To Hovington's eye, it looked like it was decorated in pseudo-modern grunge. Expensive pseudo-modern grunge. It wasn't Hovington's favorite restaurant, but he had to find someplace for lunch where they wouldn't kick Quinn out. He tended to underdress—dramatically.

Today he was wearing old blue jeans and a paint-spattered tee shirt. He had a red bandana tied back over his thin brown hair. Perfect for the Royalton. They were used to artistic types. Hovington couldn't understand why

Quinn didn't freeze to death, even wearing a heavy war surplus jacket. It had to be 15 degrees outside. Probably the alcohol. Quinn was holding his second glass of straight single malt Scotch. And it was lunchtime, for God's sake.

Hovington brushed some crumbs off the tablecloth with delicate strokes. He still wasn't exactly sure how to proceed. "I thought the reviews in the *Times* were excellent. They certainly caught the uniqueness of your work. Its importance." He looked at the tablecloth again and brushed at another stray crumb.

Another grunt.

"Uh—Essame. There's only one small thing." He decided to take the plunge.

"What?" Quinn was not your more socially adept artist. In that sense, Hovington missed Arthur DeRuk. DeRuk had been finely attuned to the social graces, at least to the extent he thought it would help him.

"The *Times* mentions your little outburst," Hovington said, looking directly at Quinn. "We love the publicity, and certainly it's expected that an artist of your caliber will be high strung." He tried an engaging smile.

Quinn's dark brown eyes flashed and his mouth tightened under the beard.

Hovington proceeded more tentatively. "But you really . . ." He started again. "I think you should be a little more cautious. You know Mimi Aaron is one of the wealthiest and most influential women in New York. Her husband—no, ex-husband—owns Witten's. She could do a lot to help you. You really shouldn't have offended her."

"Fuck her. I don't need her help. My art speaks for itself." He finished his drink in a large swallow and held up the empty glass to signal the waiter for another.

"Well, yes it does. But offending a potential patron

isn't good business. You know this is important to both of us."

Another drink appeared in front of Quinn. The waiter scurried away. Quinn took a sip and glared at Hovington.

"Essame, perhaps it would be wise to watch your drinking a bit. Particularly when we're having a show. Have you gotten your driver's license back yet?"

"None of your God damned business. You're my dealer, not my mother, asshole." Hovington received a clenched-jaw stare across the half-finished salads. Quinn reached for his glass again and took another large swallow. People in the dining room were turning to look.

"Some people were shocked at what you said about Arthur DeRuk. I know you didn't like him, but . . ."

Quinn slammed his drink down. Scotch splashed on his hand. He wiped it back and forth on the tablecloth. Now the people around them were definitely listening. Hovington lowered his voice.

"You're right, of course. DeRuk was a bastard. And he misused you." Hovington carefully avoided referring to his part in that episode. "But people don't like to hear anyone speak ill of the dead. It shocks them." Hovington sat back in his chair and folded his long arms across his chest. There. He'd said it.

"Fuck 'em," Quinn said. Heads turned.

A lady two tables away started signaling for the manager. Hovington hurried on. He'd gone this far. He might as well get it all out. He so hated unpleasantness.

"Frankly, I think it hurt the sale of your art. We only sold six pieces. That's what I mean. It's not good for either of us."

Quinn spoke in a loud voice roughened by his smoking. "DeRuk was shit. He's dead and the world's better off for it. I'm glad. Too bad it couldn't have been slower and more painful. I hated the fucker."

People were starting to get up and leave, giving them a sour look as they passed.

"Essame, that's not the point. Just try to be more circumspect, that's all I ask." Hovington noticed their waiter whispering to a large man across the room. The man turned, his face set in a frown, and started towards them.

"Fucker," Quinn muttered, drifting off into his own dark alcohol-laced thoughts.

Hovington turned his face away from Quinn and reflected on Arthur DeRuk. A thin smile pulled at his mouth.

Chapter twenty-five

Jonathan headed for the patio. He was committed to putting his problems aside, at least for the evening. Particularly since he couldn't figure out what to do.

Two men in pearl-button cowboy shirts were feeding chunks of oak into the flickering fire of a large black metal drum that had been cut in half, lengthwise, and mounted on steel legs with thick rubber tires. A grill was suspended by pulleys above it. The sun was settling into the hills in the west. A gentle breeze with a touch of cold in it brushed his face. He headed towards the heat lamp glowing near the drinks table set up on a corner of the patio.

A slim, small, blond woman, casually dressed in jeans, a cowboy shirt and a short denim jacket, walked toward him and held out her hand. She looked to be about Mimi's age. Jonathan felt out of place in his sports coat and tie.

"Well, hi. I'm Barbara Zager. We sure are glad to have you here. I was out shoppin' when you and Day got home."

Jonathan smiled at the fluid southern accent. "It's a pleasure to meet you," he said, taking the soft hand. "Do I detect an accent there?"

"Just a bit of Georgia left over in me from mah childhood," she said, smiling and speaking in a more exaggerated accent. "Ah guess it just never went away."

"It's charming. How long have you been out in California?"

"Only about forty years," she laughed, showing her even white teeth. "But you can't take the south out of a girl. Here, let me pour you some wine now." She turned and moved towards the drinks table. "What would you like? We've got some of our Pinot and Chardonnay. We think they're pretty good."

"Some Chardonnay, please." He moved with her over to the table.

"How long have you and Day been married?" he asked as she poured the pale golden wine into one of the smaller crystal wineglasses.

She turned to hand him the glass. "Oh, goin' on about forever."

They were interrupted by Day Zager together with a younger couple.

"Kandy and Aaron Budgor, this is Jonathan Franklin," Zager made the introductions. "These guys are my competition, Jonathan. They own the place down the road a ways."

"What brings you all the way out to the Santa Ynez Valley?" Kandy asked. Her voice had a pleasant effervescence. It matched her round face framed by short dark hair. He noticed the freckles across her nose, below hazel eyes that danced with humor.

"Just trying to learn something about the wine business," he said.

Barbara Zager brought her a glass of Pinot without asking. "Why, thank you, Barbara," Kandy said, swishing the wine around at eye level, sniffing it and taking a sip. "You guys sure do good stuff."

Then she turned her full attention back to Jonathan. "You came to the right place. Day and Beno know more about the wine business than anyone around here, that's for sure."

"Who's Beno?" Jonathan asked.

"Oh, that's my husband." She lifted the wineglass towards the shorter of the two men. He had a cherubic smile with a touch of devilishness around his eyes. He was deep in conversation with Day Zager, bouncing on the balls of his feet as he talked. "No one calls him Aaron," Kandy said. "Not even his mother. Day introduces him that way to pull his chain. They just love to poke at each other."

Barbara Zager came over and handed Jonathan another glass of white wine. This wine had a deeper, more vivid golden color. He could smell peach and pineapple before he got the glass all the way up to his nose. He paused as Barbara Zager continued, tipping his head sideways towards her.

"This is our 1998 Reserve Chardonnay. That was a spectacular year out here. And this wine has the sturdiness to take some aging. See if you like it."

Jonathan swirled, smelled and then sipped. He smiled broadly. "Sensational," he said enthusiastically. "This is a fabulous wine, Mrs. Zager. Thank you for sharing it."

"Now don't you go and call me Mrs. Zager anymore, you hear. I'm just Barbara. We're mighty informal out here. Just farmers plowing the land and trying to make a living."

Her words did not quite match up to the six-thou-sand-square-foot, two-story house finished in beautiful river rock and teak, or the fine linen and china setting the table at the other edge of the patio, overlooking miles of vineyards.

My God, thought Jonathan. It's December and we're sitting outside. He looked around the beautiful vineyards spilling over the hills into the gathering dusk. He was get-ting to like this investment more and more. He took another sip of the Reserve Chardonnay and smiled to himself.

Captivating smells drifted over from the barbeque. The meat sizzled and popped over the hot wood coals as the wine flowed. Jonathan relaxed.

"Y'all come and sit down now," Barbara said, making a gesture that took them all in. "Jonathan, you come over here and sit by me." She patted the back of a chair. "Kandy and I'll get to share you. The boys can sit over there next to each other. We've got some tri-tip and beans. Corn done in the fire. I sure hope you like our bar-beque. We call it Santa Maria out here."

He did. Especially the tri-tip. It turned out to be a cut of beef he'd never had before. The nip of the air gave him an appetite, and his problems slipped away to the back of his mind as he took his first moist bite.

Day Zager opened a bottle of red wine. He spoke as he worked. "This is our '99 Reserve Pinot. Usually we would serve a cabernet with barbeque, but this wine was special. Let's see if it'll hold up to the meat." He poured the ruby red wine into large tulip-shaped glasses. He passed one to Jonathan.

"Day, this may be a silly question," Jonathan said. "I've been drinking wine for thirty years, and I always wondered why we drink red wine out of bigger glasses and white out of the smaller ones." He looked around the table, realizing how much at home he felt to let his guard down like that. His question drew a laugh from the others.

Beno was the first to speak. "I think it's the glass makers, myself. I have a hard time telling the difference. Now they've even got different glasses for Bordeaux and Burgundy. They sure sell more glasses, though. It's getting to be like tennis shoes."

"Now, now, Beno," Day Zager said. "Be kind. I've known some people who say they can tell the difference in the way the wines present." He swirled some of the Pinot in his glass and spent an instant watching it. "Come to think of it though, those folks may have been from Riedel," he said, still looking at the wine. They all chuckled. "But I want to know what our guest thinks of this Pinot."

Jonathan stuck his nose in the glass after giving it a little swirl. Plum, cherry, blackberry. He tasted it and rolled a bit of the wine on his palate, staring up into the night sky. "Full, but nicely balanced," he murmured, almost to himself. "Thoroughly drinkable now, but it seems like it has a lot of structure. That's a marvelous wine," he concluded, looking directly at Day Zager. "I think that's the best Zager Pinot I've ever had. Thank you."

"We're just glad you like it," Barbara Zager said.

"Do you always live like this?" Jonathan asked, turning towards her.

"No. 'Course not." She paused with impeccable timing. "But you have to live simple sometimes, now don't you?" As she laughed, her smile seemed to light up the table.

Dinner wound down and the small conversation quieted. Pinpricks of a thousand stars pierced the black sky. Jonathan held up his glass and made a toast to his hosts. After a moment to savor the wine, he turned to Day Zager.

"Day, I'd love to know something about your business. Do you mind talking about it? This has been such a lovely dinner."

"Nope. That's why we're here. Fire away."

"What kind of costs do you have in making a wine like this Pinot?" Jonathan asked, looking up through the ruby-colored wine shimmering in the large, thin, tulip-shaped glass.

"Lots. Now we figure our grapes cost around three thousand dollars per ton. As I told you, we prune 'em back real hard to get lots of flavor. The fewer the grapes, the lower the yield, the more concentrated the flavor. That's how it works."

"It must be good soil," said Jonathan.

"Not hardly. It's rocky. That's on purpose. 'Terroir,' we call it. It gives the grapes character. They need to struggle. Rocky soil like this is great for Pinot. It took us a long time to find this land and our other vineyards. Figure out what kind of grapes to plant. That and the microclimates are the things that make the wine. Ocean breezes down the canyon and cool fogs in the hottest months in this vineyard."

Beno cut in.

"Day here doesn't know a thing about making wine, Jonathan. You listen to me. It's not about terroir. Oh, sure, you need good grapes. But the secret is what we do in the winery. How we craft the wine."

Zager laughed.

"We've been having this argument for on to twelve years now," he said. "Beno here's wrong, but he's just too darn stubborn to admit it. I guess you're going to have to decide for yourself."

"How many bottles do you get from a ton?" Jonathan asked.

"That varies, of course, but say five hundred," Zager replied. "We only use free run juice. I told you that. So it costs around six dollars a bottle for the juice alone. A French oak barrel costs about seven hundred and fifty dollars. Good American oak maybe four hundred. Going up. But figure four hundred-fifty dollars a barrel now on average. We replace fifty percent each year. That runs a dollar twenty-five to a dollar fifty a bottle. Bottle costs a buck. Cork seventy-five cents. Label including design, maybe ninety cents. Call it ten bucks a bottle. That sound about right to you, Beno?"

"Yeah. Pretty close." He nodded.

"So it's ten dollars a bottle before getting anything back for capital investment, carrying costs, labor—and boy there's a lot of that—marketing, storage. You know, all those other things." Zager took a long sip of wine.

"How much do you get?"

"There's a lot of competition out there. We need to sell the wine. Spend a lot of time setting our price point. Retail is about twice our price. We price the Reserve Pinot at about twenty-two dollars and change in a good year. But all years aren't that good. And God help us if we have a drought."

Beno interrupted again.

"That's why we say out here the only way to make a small fortune in this business is to start with a big one."

Everyone laughed. To Jonathan's ear, some of the laughter sounded a little hollow.

Chapter twenty-six

"Jonathan, it's Frankee Perone."

"Frankee, do you know what time it is?" Jonathan said groggily. He brushed his fingers through his thinning hair and yawned.

"Sure, it's 8:30."

"It's 5:30. I'm in bed asleep. The sun isn't even up."

"Where the hell are you?"

"California."

"What are you doing there?"

"I'm at a winery."

"Oh, drinking."

"No, Frankee. It's business." He fumbled on the bed-side table for his glasses.

"Sure." She didn't sound convinced. "You want me to call you back later? After you sober up."

"No. I'm awake now. And I'm not drunk." He pushed himself up against the pillows. "What's up?"

"I thought you'd like an oral on those people you

wanted me to look at. Nasty bunch you got yourself in with. I thought art was supposed to be genteel."

"Come on, Frankee. What've you got? I want to go back to sleep." He looked around for a bottle of water. His mouth felt pasty.

"My, my. We are touchy, aren't we? I haven't heard you so cranky since I criticized your tweed jacket."

"Frankee."

"Okay, okay. Here it is. This guy Arthur DeRuk looks to me like someone should have given a party when he left our world. A bad dude. He had a nasty temper. Four DUI's. You know about his heroin addiction. Entered rehab twice, the last time about five months before his death. He never got publicity he didn't like. More newspaper articles than you can count. Courted it. Arrested once for beating up one of his girlfriends. Dismissed. We think he bought her off. Constantly womanizing. It was hard to find someone who only disliked him. Let's hope it wasn't murder. Way too many suspects."

"I wonder why Mimi liked him."

"Oh, he could be charming, and he was intelligent. Some people say he was a terrific artist. Women loved him, which was part of the problem. That's what makes me wonder why he surrounded himself with such losers." She stopped. He heard her riffling through some papers.

"Go on." He shifted his position in bed and burrowed further under the covers. He had his eyes closed.

"Sorry. Trying to find something. His dealer—art dealer, not drugs—was Warren Hovington, right?"

"Uh-huh."

"He was well known, but the guy has credit problems."

"What'd you find?" Jonathan's eyes opened behind his glasses.

"There were several active lawsuits. Mostly creditors. Some from people complaining about leaving deposits and not getting delivery. He may have been putting a lot of money up his nose. We picked up rumors of a cocaine addiction."

"Hovington?"

"Yeah."

"Go on." The warm covers were starting to make him drowsy. He fought to maintain his concentration.

"It looks to me like he was scurrying around to get money from Peter to pay Paul. This one wasn't a womanizer. He liked boys, the younger the better."

"Minors?"

"No. Not that young."

"Okay."

"You also mentioned an Essame Quinn."

"Yeah. He's an artist I met. He didn't seem to like DeRuk."

"Boy, that's an understatement. Word is that DeRuk was responsible for getting him thrown out of Hovington's gallery. There was a bankruptcy and a divorce. There was a police report that Quinn threatened to kill DeRuk. He filed a complaint against Quinn for stalking, but it never went anywhere."

"Anything else?"

"Yeah. Quinn is a guy who holds a grudge. There were two arrests for assault. Barroom fights. No convictions. The charges were withdrawn."

"Sounds sweet. What else do you have?"

"The last one's a beaut. A woman named Myacura Ishii."

Jonathan reared upright on the bed. "Oh?"

"Some mental problems. Prone to violence."

A scene from *Fatal Attraction* flickered through his

mind.

"Promiscuous. Sleeps with anyone."

He was overwhelmed by a well-nurtured sense of guilt followed almost immediately by an itching in his groin. He hoped it was his imagination.

"It seems like she had a brief but very public affair with DeRuk. There were several newspaper articles on fights they had in public. According to the papers, she gave as good as she got. She wasn't a happy camper." Frankee chuckled. "She went after him with a broken champagne bottle one night. DeRuk was running for his life."

Terrific, he thought, his stomach churning. He closed his eyes and rested the back of his head against the headboard.

"Anyone else you turned up?"

"Yeah. A lawyer. DeRuk sued him for fraud, malpractice and breach of fiduciary duty. He hated DeRuk loudly and in a lot of places. Counter-sued for several hundred thousand in fees he claimed DeRuk stiffed him for. But we got nothing to indicate he was violent. Here's another one for you. An art critic from the *New York Times*. DeRuk threw a drink in his face and hit him. Broke his nose. The guy threatened to kill DeRuk. It passed over. He's essentially a pussy, according to the people we spoke to. We don't see him killing anybody. We also got a lot of women. I mean a lot. But nothing stood out. We can look closer if you want."

"Great, Frankee. Good job." Jonathan tried to respond calmly. "Send me over a written report on what you have as soon as you can. I won't be home until tomorrow night. Let's hold off on looking at those other people for now."

There was a silence on the other end of the telephone.

"Frankee. Are you there?"

"Jonathan, I may be imagining this, but I think you have a problem. You know I'm close to some people on the N.Y.P.D. They help me out unofficially."

"What are you getting at?"

"Well, I spoke to one of them about DeRuk. I was getting some good information."

"Yeah."

"Then I mentioned Mimi Aaron's name." Jonathan opened his eyes. "I wanted to see if there was any connection. I wasn't expecting much. But my source clammed up tight. I couldn't get another thing out of him. My take on it is that the police think this is a homicide. I think she's a suspect. Maybe the prime suspect. I thought you should know."

Shit, he thought as he hung up the phone. He couldn't go back to sleep. The itch in his groin had disappeared, thank God.

Chapter twenty-seven

He was sitting at the breakfast nook off the Zagers' large open kitchen, watching the sun play across the wooden tabletop. He sipped his coffee, using both hands. I could grow to like this life, he mused. Except my head hurts. That made him think about Myacura Ishii. He pushed the thought aside.

He was tired. He had risen early following the call from Frankee Perone and wandered down to the kitchen. He was pleased to find the cook already bustling about and the aroma of rich coffee brewing. Once he was seated, a plate of hot, fluffy blueberry pancakes appeared, fresh butter dripping down the sides. A pewter jug of maple syrup sat on the table.

"You want some more coffee?" she asked.

He nodded to the heavyset woman. "Please."

As he lifted the steaming cup to his lips, he felt his tension. Until Frankee's call, he hadn't thought of Mimi or his problems with Nicole, nor the bottle-wielding Myacura Ishii. Mimi was the prime suspect. Was she playing with him? He remembered her gray-green eyes, the snow in Central Park. Just as he turned his thoughts to her, he was interrupted.

"Good morning," Day Zager said, smiling broadly as he trod into the room. "Can I join you?"

"Please."

A cup of black coffee appeared in front of him as he pulled back the wooden chair and sat down. Zager nodded his thanks to the cook. Then he turned back to Jonathan.

"Hey, get going on those pancakes. Don't wait for me. Out here, you get your food, you eat it."

"Thanks," Jonathan said, pouring on syrup and taking a bite. As he savored, he managed a smile around his dark thoughts.

"Not bad, huh?"

"Terrific," Jonathan said.

Jonathan put his fork down and looked over at Zager. "What a life you lead. Is it always like this?"

Day Zager chuckled, a smile in his blue eyes.

"Sometimes," he said. "It's pretty hectic during harvest, but winters are nice. We try to stick around the house and be with friends. Mostly limit the number of wine and charity events we attend. We're pretty selective."

"Are there a lot of them?"

"More than you can imagine. I bet we get three or four calls a day from charities that want us to donate our wines or pour." He picked up his coffee and blew onto it. "And the Vintner's Association here in the valley is pretty active. It can be grueling. Hey, it looks like the sun is getting in your eyes."

Jonathan had glanced away, and Zager noticed.

"It can be pretty bright out here. The air's so pure.

Let me pull that curtain a bit." He fussed with it a little. "That okay?"

Jonathan nodded. "Why do you do it?" he asked, returning to the conversation.

"What?" said Zager.

"Give all the wine to charities. Pour for their events."

"We're a small winery. We don't have a lot of marketing money. Once the wine leaves here, it's pretty much on its own. These charity events are one of the few ways we have to get our name out there. Barbara's a big help with all that. Folks seem to like her."

"Great lady," Jonathan responded, his mind slipping to Nicole. I miss her, he thought and she hasn't called.

"Barbara's one of the best," Zager said. "We couldn't do it without her. She works hard. Most folks think she's the real brains behind this outfit." He paused. "They're right, of course."

Jonathan smiled.

"What about the ratings from Robert Parker or the *Wine Spectator*?" he asked. He forced himself to concentrate.

"Doin' great! We've been pretty lucky. We got a 95 from the *Wine Advocate* on our '99 Pinot Reserve you had last night and a 96 from the *Wine Spectator*."

"Wow." Jonathan lifted another forkful of pancakes to his mouth and savored the flavors. "Where's your breakfast?"

"I usually just have coffee. Maybe a piece of toast sometimes. Not a big breakfast eater. Besides, it helps keep the weight off."

"You're in great shape," Jonathan said, feeling his belt tug against his stomach.

"Comes from working out of doors. I slimmed down when I quit doctoring. Always something to do around here. But you asked about how we market the wines."

"Yes."

"It's really word of mouth among the wine connoisseurs that sells the wine," Zager said. "We like to refer to them as winos." He gave Jonathan a mischievous smile. "You look like a wino to me. Sound like one too."

"You got me in one," he said. "But go on about your marketing. It's one of the areas I'm interested in."

"Well, we've had no problem selling our production so far. Even have folks on allotment. But we're too small to make a lot because of our overhead. That's why I'm looking at a few hundred more acres of land to plant. We need to make more wine. But it's a long-term project. Land's gotten pretty pricey in this neck of the woods."

Jonathan pushed aside his plate. "You said in the car yesterday that you'd explain the financials to me. As I mentioned, I think there might be some issues."

"Sure there are. But maybe not the ones you think. Where do you want to start?"

"How about the balance sheet. It looked to me like there's no equity in the business."

Zager shifted in his seat to face Jonathan more directly. "Nope. That's not true. It just doesn't show up on the financials. The land, for instance. It's worth three or four times what we paid for it. Our library too."

Jonathan held up his hand. "Library?"

"Our wine library. We cellar several cases of our wine from each vintage. You know, so we can pour verticals or do special tastings. Like next week."

"Sorry?"

"I guess I didn't mention that. We're having a big barbeque here in the vineyard. Expecting around two hundred people to come out. Doing a cellar and futures sale."

"I've bought Bordeaux futures through Sherry-Lehman in New York," Jonathan said. "I didn't know you do them direct."

"We're too small to do a large futures sale. Don't have enough wine to interest the big dealers. But we can sell more than you think by doing these events right here. People just love it when we bring out older wines they can buy. Big draw. And the futures sale takes some of the pressure off the current vintage. Good business."

Pretty sophisticated too, Jonathan thought.

"Anyway, to get back to your question, our library wines go up in value. Our best wines are made to be laid down. Better with age and more valuable. The longer we're in business, the better the library."

Jonathan nodded. "Any other assets like the land and the library?"

"Well, don't forget all those barrels of wine out in the winery. They appreciate in value as we age them for sale. That's probably the biggest asset we have because there's so much of it. With a winery you have to fill up the pipeline, and then you have a couple of years of wine in the barrels all the time. Anyway, that's all shown at cost on the balance sheet. Accountants insist. Even ignoring the good will though, the business is worth a lot of money."

"So what are the issues?" Compared to mine, Jonathan thought. Like Ishii coming after him with a broken wine bottle or Mimi being a cold-blooded killer.

"Income and cash flow."

"How so?"

"Our costs are high. You saw how much the wine costs just in raw materials. What with labor, there's not much left for overhead and marketing. Much less profit. And it's sort of like the movie business. Winemaking is so appealing, lots of rich people want to be in it, even if there's no money. It's the lifestyle. Nothin' like it for one of those Hollywood folks mentioning how they happen to own a winery. They come and go, but it makes it difficult for the rest of us."

"Speaking of rich people, I'm curious. How did Simon get involved in the winery?"

Day chuckled. "Oh, call it marketing. Simon's an old friend. I've known him since college."

"Marketing? You're kidding. This one I've got to hear." As he smiled, he thought about Mimi. He wondered if Simon was doing some other, more adroit marketing—of Mimi's innocence, perhaps.

Chapter twenty-eight

"Well, it was pretty soon after I bought the winery," Day Zager continued.

The cook came out of the kitchen, looked down at the table and shook her head at the half-eaten stack of pancakes. She looked up at Jonathan. "You didn't like 'em?"

"Gosh, no. I mean yes. They were great. I'm just trying to watch my waistline."

She snorted and picked up the plate. "You want anything else, Mr. Zager?"

He shook his head. "No. Thanks."

She waddled away, muttering.

Zager laughed. "We'd all weigh 300 pounds if it were up to her. Anyway, about Simon. I was trying to figure out how to get our name known. I thought we were making some pretty good wine. But no one was paying us much attention. You know, I've always liked Simon. We used to get together whenever he was around here. What with his plane, he seemed to drop by pretty regularly. So one evening we were playing poker . . ."

"Poker?"

"Yep. Regular game. When Simon was here, I asked him if he wanted to sit in. So we were playing and I got these three aces. Simon and I were the only ones left in the pot. He was being aggressive like he always is, and it was kind of pissing me off. I'll bet you didn't know he can be a real asshole sometimes." His blue eyes twinkled.

"I've noticed," Jonathan deadpanned.

"He had just acquired Witten's and he was getting a lot of publicity," Zager went on. "He was becoming pretty well known among a lot of well-connected people. The kind of people who like good wine and talk about it."

Jonathan got up and pulled the curtains closed to block the flood of sunshine. "Sorry, go on."

"Well, Simon was getting mentioned in the news-paper a lot. So it occurred to me to bet him 20% of the winery against 1% of Witten's. At best, I figured I would shut him up. Which would be a change. And even if I lost, the winery wasn't worth a hell of a lot then, and I figured as how we would get a slew of attention in the press. Good story, don't you think?"

"Absolutely. So what happened?"

"The son of a bitch had a six-high straight. It's not that I minded losing. It's that he was so damn cocky. Right up until I made the first capital call, that is. We put in a fair bunch of money then. Whooee. You should have heard the caterwauling. You'd a thought I had scraped the man's last meal right off his plate. Been like that for the last few years too. He's been bitching ever since. And wait 'til we start buying more land and expanding production. Must be why he laid off some of his share on you."

"Look, Day, all this is interesting," Jonathan said.

"Let me think through the financial stuff. Maybe I'll have some ideas that could be useful. I'll give you a call."

Zager put his hands on his knees and struggled to his feet, letting out a low groan. "Damn trouble with getting old," he said. "Get stiff in all the wrong places." He let that ride for a beat. "Well, when you're ready to go back out to the airport, I'll drive you. Just give a holler. Got some things to do out in the winery, if you'll excuse me."

"You know, one thing's been bothering me," Jonathan said.

"Oh?"

"You don't sound much like an Easterner." The question had been rattling around in his head since he'd met the former New York doctor.

"Folks out here don't trust to do business too much with people that sound like that. Sort of like changing uniforms when you change teams."

"Sure. Makes sense." He understood. He'd changed uniforms, from pinstripes to tweeds, when he'd left Wall Street and gone to teach in Cambridge.

"Took me a few years to assimilate," Zager said.

"Maybe the folks out here are on to something," Jonathan said, thinking ruefully of Simon.

Chapter twenty-nine

Simon Aaron's plane lifted off effortlessly and climbed out over the Santa Barbara Channel. As it leveled off, the co-pilot opened the door of the cockpit and stepped out.

"Hello, again. I thought you might like to know what's happening."

"Sure." Jonathan reached over and picked up the tweed jacket he had thrown on the opposite seat. "Sit down."

"Thanks. Well, our flight plan calls for us to head out over Las Vegas and then turn on a course that'll take us a little north of Kansas City. We'll make good time. It should be pretty smooth, except for some bad weather in the Midwest that's rolling down from Canada. We've requested clearance to climb to 45,000 feet, so we should miss the worst of it. I'll let you know if you should buckle up. Can I get you anything?"

Jonathan shook his head. "I've got some work to do."

* * *

The whine of the engines dropped him into a curtain of white noise that came close to silence. He loosened his tie and rolled up his sleeves. He pulled down the window shade and settled back into the soft gray leather seat, swiveling it back and forth with the ball of his foot. At 500 knots, he had four and a half hours to think.

Christ, he mused. Anyone looking at me would think I have everything. I'm rich. Maybe not by Simon's standards or even Nicole's. But I'm rich. I have a great house. I'm a professor at the best law school in the world. And I have a wonderful woman. And look what I've managed to make of it. Shit.

That thought led him back to Myacura Ishii. The woman was nuts. Maybe dangerous. Then he caught the echo of how she had felt moving under him. He pushed it away, horrified with himself. His fist struck the armrest. "You're an asshole, Professor," he murmured. Think. Think.

Frankee Perone's call. This DeRuk thing was more serious than Mimi realized. He was doing his best not to be irritated with her. She seemed to be a good-hearted woman, but damn it, she wasn't being smart about this. Assuming she was innocent. Dark events were darkening down his thoughts.

He picked up the airphone from the polished wooden ledge. He needed to speak to Simon. Share the pain.

"Jonathan. Good to hear from you. How's Day Zager?"

"Just great. But I called to talk about Mimi. I'm worried."

"Why?" It sounded more like "Why now?"

"I spoke with Frankee Perone this morning. I got her to do some background work on DeRuk, as you suggested."

"So?"

"She thinks the police regard DeRuk's death as suspicious and Mimi as a suspect. I think we've got to get Mimi a criminal lawyer."

"It's okay with me, but I don't think Mimi's going to buy it."

"I don't know. She's scared. The police are interviewing the people around her. And she doesn't have an alibi."

"Do you think a criminal lawyer will help?"

Jonathan stared at the gleaming wood for a moment. "To tell you the truth, I don't know. She's already talked to the police. Maybe a criminal lawyer could come up with a strategy."

"I know the woman. She didn't do anything wrong, and she'll be damned if she's going to get a criminal lawyer. It'd be a kind of admission. She'll want you to solve it."

Jonathan took in the words like a desert takes rain. He didn't want to dwell on paranoid thoughts of Mimi as a diabolical killer. "Simon, this isn't what I signed up for. What're we going to do?" He didn't try to hide his exasperation.

"What are the chances of getting the police to focus on someone else?"

"Not good. Not unless we can give them some reason to. Right now, they're focused on Mimi."

"Hang on for a second. Lauren needs something." Simon must be in the office early, Jonathan realized. The phone went dead for a moment. "Sorry, but she wouldn't interrupt unless it was urgent."

"No problem."

"About the police, what if we could get them some information on other people? You know, motive, means, opportunity, that sort of TV stuff."

That's deep, Jonathan thought. "There were plenty of people who hated DeRuk's guts. Frankee even found a couple who threatened his life. But for whatever reason, the police don't seem interested."

"Do you think it's because Mimi is rich and well known? Is some cop trying to make a name for himself?"

"Maybe, Simon, but I don't think so. Frankee says the homicide cop on this is pretty solid."

"Why not call Frankee and get her to dig around some more?"

"I can do that. I sure don't know what else to do. I'll also talk to Mimi about a criminal lawyer. Maybe you should speak to her too."

Simon sighed. "I will."

Jonathan got up to use the restroom. The plane hit a bump and his arm banged into an empty seat. He felt uneasy being alone in a plane that was configured comfortably for twelve. Being rich wasn't all it was cracked up to be.

"Frankee. Jonathan."

"Swell." She didn't sound overjoyed.

"Frankee, I need you to do some more work on the DeRuk matter."

"What?"

"I need to know where everyone was during the 24 hours before Mimi discovered DeRuk's body." He pushed his glasses back up on his nose.

"We don't do alibi kinds of stuff. That's pure police work. It uses up a lot of time. We're primarily into corporate matters now."

"Frankee, I need this. Even the three people—Hovington, Quinn and Ishii—would be useful. I really need some help trying to keep Mimi Aaron out of trouble." He waited a beat. "This is a personal request from Simon Aaron." The implied threat was clear.

There was silence on the other end of the telephone. Simon Aaron was an important man. A powerful client no one would choose to offend. As opposed to, say, a middle-aged law professor. Jonathan waited it out. The silence screamed.

"You know, Jonathan, every time you call me you become a pain in the ass. We've been friends a long time. I'm going to do this. But it's going to cost you."

"What?"

"Another thirty-five."

"Do it. When can you have the information?"

"Depends. First I'll see if I can get it from my NYPD contacts. I doubt it. If not, we'll have to do the legwork. Give me the time period we're looking at."

"Mimi discovered the body on November 1. That means we're looking at Halloween. Say one p.m. on the 31st to noon the next day."

"We'll get on it."

"Call me, Frankee. Soon."

Chapter thirty

The weather was as dour as his mood. Rain stippled the windows, and the sky was a tattered gray blanket hanging off the tops of the tallest buildings. Jonathan had just gotten back into the city. He was pacing the living room of Nicole's apartment on Central Park West, thoughts of Myacura Ishii, primal and fearful by turn, driving his anxieties.

He went over to the couch and sank into its plush embroidered pillows. He was getting too damned old to be in this kind of trouble.

He got up to pace the room again, his hand rubbing the small silver snuffbox in his pocket that his father had given him. He looked out the window at the park. The effect of the lights filtering through the bare trees resembled a stark Chinese landscape painting. He glanced at the French Regency clock on the mantel. Two minutes since he had looked at it last.

Ishii. She was a mistake. That kind of thing just happens.

It wouldn't happen again, he assured himself. But he was uncertain in some small part of him whether it was true.

He went into the den and picked up the telephone. He dialed Simon's home number and got no response. Then he dialed Harv Champlin.

"Harv. I'm glad I caught you. It's Jonathan."

Harvey Champlin was his old friend and former protégé. He was now a partner at Whiting & Pierce, the most important and powerful of the white-shoe Wall Street law firms. Jonathan's old firm.

"Hey, buddy, it's good to hear your voice. What's up?"

"I was wondering if you want to have dinner tonight?"

"Love to, but no way. I've got three deals working. Looks like another all-nighter for me. But let's make it soon. I'd love to catch up."

"Sure thing." Jonathan kept it light. "I'm not sure what my schedule is right now. Let me get back to you when I get it figured out."

"Great. I'd look forward to that. Have a terrific evening."

Harv had sounded so into it, like he was riding the curl of the wave. It brought back memories. He missed it. Before going off to teach at Harvard five years ago, Jonathan had been one of the hottest young partners there. He had burned out on big deals, and his father's death had caused him to rethink his life. At the moment he wasn't so sure he'd made the right decision. He kept worrying the little snuffbox until it grew warm in his hand.

He sighed and struggled into his jacket and topcoat. He was jet-lagged but too buzzed to stay inside. He paused to turn out the light, looking back into the dark room. He usually loved the time between Thanksgiving and Christmas. Usually. Not this year.

He remembered he still hadn't bought Nicole a Christmas present. Now he wondered if it would be necessary. The thought drove him deeper into his dark mood.

He hailed a cab. Smith & Wollensky, at Third and 49th was one of his favorite restaurants. The old wood dining rooms bustled with the electricity of groups of young lawyers and investment bankers bantering loudly. The steaks were first-rate and the wine list was grand, if a little pricey. He hoped the atmosphere would cheer him up. But even as the maitre d' waved him to a table in his practiced way, Jonathan still felt down. He shrugged off his jacket and pulled down his tie as the maitre d' held out his chair.

The waiter had just uncorked a bottle of '89 Pichon Lalande and left him to his thoughts. Tables for one were getting tough again as the city slowly shook off 9/11 like a great animal emerging from its winter lair. It had been a year. He was glad to see the place full. This table was in the back corner upstairs, which was just fine with him in his brooding frame of mind. He took off his glasses and rubbed his fingers against the bridge of his nose.

Nicole has just been away a few days, and look what has happened. My relationship is in deep shit because I'm scared to death to have a kid. And God help me if Mya-cura Ishii gets in touch with her. What's wrong with my head? Nicole's a terrific lady. I'll never find anyone better. At least anyone who'll put up with me.

Still, the thought of a child made him squirm. Why am I so afraid of having a child? he asked himself. Himself didn't answer.

He sipped his wine, fretting, mind churning.

I've got a Business School dean I've never met who hates my guts. Now I don't even have the one course that was really fun to teach. Next quarter's going to be a bitch.

The waiter brought his sliced red heirloom tomatoes layered with buffalo mozzarella and glistening with a drizzle of extra virgin olive oil. "Would you like pepper, sir?" he asked in his cheerful voice, holding out a large wooden grinder. When Jonathan shook his head, he moved away. Jonathan's mind took another turn.

I haven't done much for Mimi, that's for sure. If DeRuk's death wasn't an accident, she's the most likely suspect. That's what Frankee had said. It didn't look so good.

His lawyer's mind finally stirred as he began to consider the issues. He wished that Mimi had told him about that fraud suit before Lieutenant Wayne sprung it on them. And all the other evidence out there.

Maybe the rich are different. F. Scott Fitzgerald got it right. Or at least the very rich. A fraud lawsuit wouldn't have slipped his mind. Maybe Frankee'll come up with someone else. Quinn and Myacura Ishii sure hated DeRuk's guts. He wiped a spot of olive oil from his chin with the big linen napkin. Let's hope.

He let go of that thread and picked up another as his steak arrived. "Medium, sir. Will that be all?"

He hardly noticed the rich taste as he chewed. I guess I'd better make a date with Simon to tell him about Zager. How in God's name did I let him lay off that stock on me? I own five percent of a winery that's likely to wring me dry. Bottom line, I didn't ask the right questions. Just great for such a supposedly smart lawyer.

Maybe I'm slipping.

Chapter thirty-one

"Hey, Mister, you want onions on your hot dogs?"

Simon Aaron had invited Jonathan to dinner at one of his favorite spots, a small hot dog stand in Queens, heated indoor seating in the back. They were standing at the window waiting for their dinner.

Real New York and classic Simon Aaron. It was always an adventure having dinner with Simon. He wasn't your typical billionaire. He was dressed in his familiar dark blue suit with red pinstripes under a deep blue cashmere overcoat. His Savile Row tailor did a good job with his short, pudgy body. The funny thing was, he didn't look out of place. Even with a bottle of Zager Reserve Pinot Noir sticking out of his coat pocket.

They settled down at their table covered in red waxed cloth with their paper cups and steaming hot dogs. Simon placed the wine on the table between them. With a flourish he pulled a waiter's corkscrew out of his jacket pocket, opened the wine and tasted it approvingly.

"A perfect complement to our meal. You're fortunate to be an owner," he said, pouring half a paper cup for Jonathan. "Now tell me how Day is doing and what's happening with our investment."

Jonathan bit into his hot dog. He swallowed and took a sip of wine. "Day's great. He seems to be doing exactly what he likes. As far as I can tell, it's quite a life. That's some winery." Jonathan paused. "Did he really lose 20% of it to you in a poker game?"

"Yeah, he bet into a straight. Didn't even seem upset. Strange."

Jonathan bit his tongue.

"I didn't know the financial condition," Simon continued. He put some more mustard on his second hot dog. "Great mustard they have here," he said, pointing to the bottle.

"The winery," Jonathan said.

"Yeah. Okay. I took the bet on a lark. Besides, it was the best hand I'd seen all night. What do you think, now that you've had a chance to look over the place? They sure make a great wine," he said, sniffing his paper cup as if he were ensconced in a booth at Lutece.

"I think it's not as bad as we assumed. A lot of the value is off the books in wine inventory and appreciated land value. His cash is tight, but it seems to me like he's got it under control. They had a fraud problem, but it looks like they've got it resolved. He still doesn't have enough volume to cover his overhead. He's buying more acreage, but it'll be years before the vines start producing."

"Oy," Simon said. "That means he'll be asking us for more money." That "us" again.

Jonathan ignored him. "Day went over his expenses with me," he continued. "I made a few suggestions that might help." He heard himself explaining the situation, but his mind felt leaden. He was exhausted. Sleep had eluded him last night.

"Like what? Will it save us money?" Simon wiped some mustard from his mouth.

"Well, you know that a merger of similar companies cuts down on back office overhead. It's one of the ways you've made your money."

Simon nodded with a grunt, chewing.

"Day doesn't have any interest in selling or buying, but I suggested to him that maybe he should think about a joint operating agreement."

"Remind me," said Simon.

"It's used in the newspaper business mostly, where there are two newspapers in town. They combine back office operations but keep independent newsrooms and editorial control. They both make more money."

"Okay."

"There are lots of superb small wineries in the valley, just like Zager. But they all have problems competing with the giants. They have trouble getting their names out and turning a profit while they still handcraft small batch wines."

"Okay."

"So I suggested they establish a central business office and maybe even combine some of their marketing budgets under a common over-branding, like the small high-end French champagne houses did with their 'Special Club' wines."

"Good idea. How did he react?"

"He was gracious. Whether he'll follow through, I don't know. I guess it depends on how tight things get."

Simon finished his second hot dog. "Do you want any dessert? They got great peach pie. They make it here."

"No, thanks. I'm watching my weight."

"Yeah. Me too." He sounded disappointed. "Are you making any progress with Mimi's thing?"

"None. I really need to get more information."

"Did you hire Frankee Perone? I told you, I'll pay." Simon shook his head. "Mimi causes me no end of concern. Damn it. I'd divorce her if I hadn't already."

"That reminds me," Jonathan said, "you owe me $35,000. And Frankee wants another $35,000. She's gotten expensive."

"Shit." Simon reached for his checkbook.

Jonathan hesitated. Did he really want to get into this? "Er, Simon, speaking of women problems, can I talk to you as a friend?"

Simon paused with his pen in mid-air and looked up at him. "What's up?"

"It's about Nicole."

"Oh."

"Nicole wants to have a baby."

"Uh-oh."

"I don't know what to do. I love her. I want us to be together. God knows I'll never find anyone better. But this is driving me nuts. I'm almost 51. When the kid is 14, I'll be 65. I feel like it's some sort of a jail sentence." He spread his hands in front of him as if he could pluck the answers out of the air. "I don't know why I feel that way. It's not as if I'll have to keep working. I did all right when I practiced. I've got a fair amount of money tucked away. And Nicole's rich. It's dumb, but that's just how it feels."

"It's nice of you to ask me, but you've got the wrong guy. I can't explain women. That much I know. Nicole's the most ambitious woman I ever met. Even after she got wealthy, she kept on pushing. I never thought she wanted kids." He finished writing the check and held it out to Jonathan. "Mimi and I could never have kids. You're going to have to solve this one for yourself."

Jonathan gave Simon a desperate look.

Chapter thirty-two

It was one of those mornings when the cold wind off the East River cut right through his clothes, no matter how many layers he had on. He shivered. His shoes were cold and soggy. It hadn't been such a good idea to walk across the park.

Jonathan hadn't slept well again. He had hoped the walk would help wake him up. He hunched forward into his topcoat and buried his hands deeper into his pockets as he crunched the last few steps into Mimi Aaron's building on Fifth Avenue. He wondered why she had insisted on meeting so early. It sounded urgent.

Mimi's apartment offered its familiar warmth and flower fragrance. They were seated across from each other in the living room. Jonathan had slipped off his shoes at the door.

Mimi sipped at her coffee, her gray-green eyes fixed

on him. There was something in her gaze he couldn't quite decipher. But it was different. The urgency seemed to have passed. "I appreciate your coming so quickly. There's something I wanted you to see."

She reached into a drawer in the table and took out a letter. She set it down between them. She made a graceful gesture with her hand. "This came yesterday afternoon. It appears to be important," she said. "It's very upsetting."

Her face was calm, giving no visible clues that she was upset.

"What's it about?" His tone was snappish. He still was pissed with Mimi for not squaring with him. It didn't seem to bother her.

She turned the letter around and slid it across to him, still watching his eyes. The address was handwritten and he didn't recognize the writing. He took the letter out of the envelope and skimmed it quickly. His jaw dropped.

"My God!" His face started to flush. He could feel the warmth rising in his cheeks.

"It appears you have a problem." Her words were edged.

Then her composure failed and she burst out laughing. She put a delicate hand up to her mouth. "You scamp! What were you trying to do, worm the information out of her?"

"Uh—let me try to explain."

"Yes, that would be a good idea. Is this your idea of working undercover? I very rarely receive letters from wronged women who think I should know the kind of man I'm involved with."

"Right." He was now blushing furiously. He had rarely felt so foolish. "I made a little mistake."

"I'll say." She laughed at Jonathan's discomfort, getting back some of her own. "But why in heaven's name is Myacura Ishii writing me?"

"Maybe she saw us together at the gallery opening and jumped to conclusions." He was guessing.

"Yes, possibly that's it. It's the kind of mistake she could easily make. She'd like to hurt me."

"Why?"

"Do you remember what I told you about having a fight with Arthur when I found out he was seeing another woman?"

"Yes."

"The other woman was Myacura Ishii."

"Frankee Perone told me Ishii had dated DeRuk," Jonathan said. "I had no idea she knew you."

"When Arthur broke off their relationship and we made up, she blamed me. I got a poison pen letter from her. It was vile. The woman is completely crazy."

Tell me about it, he thought, looking down at his socks.

"I'm sorry, Jonathan. I should have told you before asking you to talk to her. Of course," Mimi paused and smiled, "I didn't imagine that you'd take your job so seriously."

Jonathan cleared his throat.

"Uh, Mimi."

"Yes."

"I'd appreciate it if we kept this between us." He realized he might have dodged a bullet. At least he hoped so. Maybe Myacura Ishii thought she had taken her revenge.

"Don't worry. You keep my secrets and I'll keep yours. That's the way it works if we're going to be friends." She put her hand on his arm.

"Mimi. One more thing." He looked deeply into her eyes. "How much do you think Myacura Ishii hates you?"

Chapter thirty-three

"Arthur DeRuk couldn't paint," Warren Hovington said. "He couldn't even draw very well. He prided himself on it." Hovington's office was too hot. Jonathan felt a trickle of sweat run down his side. He had journeyed down to SoHo to the gallery. "He certainly never lifted a finger to a piece of metal. I was the intermediary with the people who fabricated his sculptures." Hovington straightened his French cuffs.

They were in a small well-appointed office behind the public gallery spaces. The walls were covered in yellow-striped silk. A major Egon Schiele oil dominated the room. The only window in the office framed Hovington's thin shoulders, long head and ponytail. Antique demi-tasse cups sat on the elegant English partners' desk that separated them. Not a single sheet of paper was in evidence.

"He wasn't an artist?" Jonathan was puzzled.

"Of course he was an artist. How can you understand what I need to do as Arthur's art executor unless you understand Arthur's art?" Hovington's thin mouth sagged in disapproval.

"Please. I'm here to learn," Jonathan said mildly, wondering how Hovington would survive one of his advanced JD/MBA seminars.

"Arthur was a conceptualist." Hovington said. "He conceptualized a piece. He took a form he found, imagined it in another material to deepen its context and placed it in a space to bring out its deepest meaning. Then his fabricators would execute the concept. Of course, I supervised them. I instructed them and dealt with them in every way. That was my job. I oversaw everything Arthur did." Hovington offered a self-satisfied smile. "But he made certain that each piece realized his vision."

Jonathan wondered whether art dealers actually learned to talk that way in school. "That's art?" He was trying to keep the disbelief out of his voice. He didn't know how well he was succeeding. He picked up his demitasse of espresso. It was cold.

"Professor Franklin. . . " The telephone on Hovington's desk rang and he reached for it. "Excuse me." He murmured a few words, then looked up. "I'm sorry, I have to take this call. It will only be a moment." He punched a button on the telephone. "Mrs. Stanley, the piece you have is one of Quinn's best. It's a marvelous piece." He listened. "Yes." He turned his back on Jonathan with a swish of his long silver ponytail. "Of course, if you must. I'm sorry it didn't please you. May I send another work for your approval?" His shoulders straightened. "I see," he said. "Then perhaps you can have the piece returned to the gallery. Thank you." He turned and replaced the receiver more firmly than necessary.

"Where were we?" he said. There was a trace of temper in his voice.

"You were about to explain DeRuk's art to me."

"Yes." He glanced down at his gold watch. "Well, Professor Franklin, it is often as important in modern and contemporary art to understand the idea behind the piece as it is to observe the piece itself. It is that tension between the idea and the execution that underlies so much of modern artistic expression. Do you know who Marcel Duchamp is?"

"Kind of. I remember his name from art appreciation in college."

"He was a founder of the Dadaist school around 1910." Hovington's tone was pedantic. "He conceived of the idea of Found Art. If his eye identified an everyday object as art, since he was an artist, that made the object art."

"Now I remember." Jonathan snapped his fingers. "A bicycle wheel or something."

"Correct. That was one piece. But a purer form for which he was justly famous was the urinal signed 'J. Mutt.' He hung it on the wall of an art show in 1912. It caused a furor in Paris."

As well it might, thought Jonathan.

"But wasn't he also an accomplished painter?" Jonathan asked. "I think I remember some of his art in the Philadelphia Museum."

"Yes."

"Let's circle back for a minute. It's the intellectual idea that's art. A urinal."

"Correct."

"If I found the same urinal and hung it on the wall, would that be art?"

"Of course not." His hand swept the idea aside. "You

are not an artist. And besides, it would no more be art than a perfect copy of a Van Gogh painting would be. Only the original is art, that which encompasses the original spark of genius."

"Then I'm still confused. DeRuk didn't create pieces. He 'imagined' them?"

"Yes." Hovington was looking down at his long, delicate fingers.

"I suppose under that theory, you could have a blank canvas representing the futile emptiness of life before it was filled with art," Jonathan laughed.

Hovington looked up sharply with surprise in his blue eyes. "I see you are familiar with Arthur's work. That piece sold for $87,000 in the Witten's spring sale."

Jonathan looked hard at Hovington's face to see if he was having his leg pulled. "You must be kidding."

"I never 'kid,' as you say, about art, Professor Franklin. It is much too important. Although Arthur had a very warped sense of humor and he wasn't a very nice man, he was an important artist."

"But how can DeRuk's art—which is really about intellectualizing a piece—be original art? That spark comes from Duchamp. Isn't DeRuk's art a copy, so to speak? Not of the piece, but of the intellectual expression."

"Perhaps you don't understand art," Hovington said. "All modern art is an intellectual expression. Execution is not important. Critically, an artist is free to do as he wishes. People will pay hundreds of thousands of dollars for a piece of DeRuk sculpture." He glanced down at his watch again.

"Perhaps I'll have better luck understanding what an art executor does."

"Of course. As Arthur's art executor, it is my duty to protect his legend. To nurture it and to make it grow. I will seek to secure Arthur's place as a great artist . . ."

"Forgive me, Mr. Hovington, but what specifically do you do? How do you relate to Mimi Aaron as the executor of the DeRuk estate?"

Hovington sighed and leaned back in his chair. He crossed his long legs and smoothed his trousers.

"I manage Arthur's art and maintain it." He held up his hand palm up, then let it collapse back into his lap. "It is my responsibility to dispose of it at the right time and in the right way. I also will create a catalog raisonne of Arthur's work."

"A book of everything he created?" Jonathan remembered the term from his work with Witten's four years ago.

"Yes, that's correct." Hovington sounded surprised.

"Isn't that a huge amount of work?"

"Of course, but as Arthur's art executor I feel obligated to his ongoing reputation to accomplish it. No one is better able to do so. And if I may say so, no one ever will be. There will be a standard in the future against which all purported pieces of Arthur's work will be judged." He straightened in his chair. "It is essential." His ponytail bobbed a little in affirmation.

"I thought the estate didn't have any money?"

"That's true, but I feel so strongly about my obligation to Arthur that I told Mrs. Aaron I would defer my fees."

"Beyond the catalog raisonne, you determine when and how DeRuk's art is sold?"

"Yes. It's a process that may take many years. The fragile nature of art, not only physical but intellectual, requires the greatest care. Of course once a specific piece has been sold, I have no further concern for that piece." He made a small gesture of its unimportance with the back of his hand. "The money is then dealt with by the executor."

"I see," said Jonathan. That wasn't the full sentence. The full sentence was "I see this guy is really full of shit and I need to find out a lot more," most of which sounded only inside his head.

Chapter thirty-four

"Mimi, I don't like this."

Jonathan was again on the couch in Mimi's Fifth
Avenue apartment. The weather had turned ugly, and
freezing rain spattered the windows. Not even the masses
of yellow tulips brightened the mood. She was sitting
across from him, her graceful hands folded in her lap.
Her eyes had a hunted look.

"This homicide detective, Lieutenant Wayne, is dangerous," he continued. "You know the police think there's
something wrong about Arthur DeRuk's death. If they
think this was murder, you're the prime suspect. In fact,
you're the only suspect. We need to get you a criminal
lawyer."

"What will he do for me, Jonathan?" Worry lines
etched her brow.

He felt a flood of relief. At least she's willing to consider it. "Well . . ." But he was stumped when he thought
it through. All a criminal lawyer could do at this point

was to make sure Mimi didn't talk to the police. She'd already talked to the police. He had mentioned strategy to Simon. That was moot now, after what Frankee Perone had told him. Only the facts mattered. He made a gesture of surrender and settled back on the couch.

"I've been completely honest. The police must know that."

"I know you've been honest. I just don't think Lieutenant Wayne believes you."

"Well, what can I do about it?" She got up and poured herself a glass of water from the carafe on the coffee table. "You yourself said everyone has an alibi."

That was the hard one. Frankee Perone had called this morning. That call was the reason for his visit. Quinn, Hovington, Myacura Ishii—all three of the most likely people who might have killed DeRuk—had airtight alibis. Really airtight.

Frankee had talked to the young stockbroker Hovington had picked up at the gallery and spent the night with. He hadn't left Hovington until late the next day. He seemed pleased with his conquest of a sophisticated older man. Frankee couldn't see any reason he would be lying. It certainly didn't do him any good. And he had met Hovington that one time. He never even wanted to know why her people were asking questions.

Quinn had apparently had a screaming match with his ex-wife over alimony and gone on a very public binge. He had ended up in the drunk tank. That was going to be a hard alibi to break.

Myacura Ishii had been working on locking down the latest *Vogue* issue and had been at her office with fourteen other people for the entire 24-hour period. It had been confirmed four different times. Maybe she had slipped away, but nobody remembered. And it was tough because there were so many people working on the lockdown. They were having a lot of problems. Someone should have noticed the absence of the assistant art director for three-quarters of an hour. Frankee had said that was the minimum time it would have taken for her to get from the magazine offices to DeRuk's apartment and back. Probably longer. And that didn't even allow time for the murder.

So there they were. No one else, at least no one obvious, could have committed the crime.

"It'd be funny if it weren't so damn scary," he said. "Everyone in the world seems to have an alibi but you." No wonder the police were concentrating on Mimi. Terrific. What the hell was he going to do now?

"Okay, forget about alibis." He waved the alibis away. "Let's assume someone faked it or there's something we don't know." Fat chance. "What about access? Who had access to DeRuk's apartment?"

"Jonathan," Mimi said. Her voice was worn. "Everyone had access." She got up and wandered to the window and stared out at the rain. "Everybody had a key. Arthur was like that. He wanted to be, I guess, open. Forgive the pun. He gave out keys to his apartment like samples at a bake sale. If he took a liking to someone, he gave them a key and told them to drop around anytime they wanted." She rejoined Jonathan, her delicate hands moving, grasping for the truth. "His apartment was always full of men and young girls and strange people coming and going. It was a constant party."

"What a guy," Jonathan said dryly.

"Then about every six months," she said, "Arthur would have the locks changed. You'd know you were still his friend if he called you to mention it. Even that girl, Myacura Ishii, had a key. Of course Warren Hovington had a key. He was always there. He acted like a brooding hen. Maybe the only one who didn't have a key was Essame Quinn. But he would have had no problem getting a key if he set his mind to it. Besides, how can we be sure someone didn't just knock on the door? Or that Arthur didn't leave the door unlocked? He did that sometimes." She looked down at her half full glass of water. "Goodness, I've been so rude. Can I get you something?"

"No, it's okay." He shifted uncomfortably. "But damn it, Mimi, that leaves us nowhere! Everyone had an alibi. Everyone had a key. Anyone could have done it. We don't even know if anyone did do it. It could have been an accident. God, at this point I hope so. It might even have been suicide. There's just no place to start."

They sat without speaking, Mimi looking out the big picture windows, her eyes unfocused, her hands fingering the pearls around her neck. Finally she broke the silence.

"There's only one thing to do," she said. "Find Rufus."

Jonathan goggled. He sat forward as he spoke. "What? The dog? Are you out of your mind?" His voice was rising. "He's probably dead. Even if he's alive, how do you start to look for a dog? He certainly wouldn't be wearing a tag. No one's that stupid. He could be anywhere within a hundred miles. He's not going to check in and ask to be sent home, you know."

"No," said Mimi with assurance. "He's not dead. Rufus was too cute for anyone to kill. I don't believe anyone could have been that cruel."

Mimi had her jaw set in a way that Jonathan had learned to identify. Stubborn. "I have an idea," she said.

She walked across to the front door, opened it, and stepped across the hallway to the only other apartment on the floor. Jonathan saw her knock. A gangly child of about eleven opened the door. He thought it was a girl, but it was hard to tell. Mimi stepped inside and the door closed. She came back about five minutes later.

"Good," she said. Then she filled in an incredulous Jonathan Franklin on what she had in mind.

Chapter thirty-five

The kid looked like a castoff from a homeless shelter. Torn jeans, ragged shirt and purple-streaked red hair. She had a spatter of freckles across her nose. They fit her bright blue eyes. No one, not ever, Jonathan was sure, would have fingered her as the daughter of one of Manhattan's most affluent and influential hedge fund managers. His thoughts were broken up by Mimi's introduction.

Mimi's eyes were shining with affection. "Daniella, this is Professor Jonathan Franklin." They were in Mimi's living room again early the next day. The sun was shining. What crazy weather they were having. Jonathan struggled up out of the deep chair in which he was sitting. "He's helping me with the problem I told you about," Mimi said.

The eleven-year-old held out a little grubby hand. Jonathan shook it, looking over Daniella's shoulder at Mimi with a skeptical expression.

"I asked Daniella how we should go about finding Rufus." She turned towards the redheaded little girl.

"Daniella, would you like a soda or some chocolate?"

"No thank you, Mrs. Aaron," Daniella replied in a polite, small voice totally at odds with her appearance.

"Have you given some thought to how we can go about finding Rufus, dear?"

"Oh, yes. When we lost Meow, our cat—his real name was Meow Zedong, you know—" she said breathlessly, "we did a lot of things. I put up posters all over the neighborhood and had Mom drive me all around."

Jonathan smirked. Just what he expected from an eleven-year-old. Mimi was off the deep end on this one. She gave him a frown of warning.

"Well, dear, we don't think Rufus is in the neighborhood. He could be anywhere, but we think he's in New York or maybe even Connecticut. Can you think of anything else we might do?"

"Sure," came the prompt reply, "we can use the Internet. It's cool." Her purple-streaked hair bounced as she spoke. "I can download all the e-mail addresses from the New York and Connecticut Veterinary Associations, and then I can compose an e-mail with a description of Rufus and put it through a program to e-mail it to all of them simultaneously. Then I can have Nicholas. . ." She turned her bright blue eyes on Jonathan. "He's my little brother. He's only nine," she said. "I can get him to search all the websites of all the animal shelters. They post pictures of all the dogs they pick up. I'll have him look at the back files. Even he can do that."

Jonathan was reminded of the husband walking alone in the forest, who by chance voiced an opinion. Was he still wrong? Ask any wife. It looked like they started early.

"There can't be that many pugs," Daniella continued

in her quick little voice. "We'll look every day. I like to use my computer. My friends—I have a lot of friends, you know. We can have a sleepover. They can bring their laptops. We'll all look." She clapped her small grubby hands together. "It'll be neat."

Jonathan realized his mouth was hanging open. He felt like an idiot. Was this kid a computer genius or were they all like this?

"I think those are wonderful ideas, dear. And we appreciate your help. Here's the $10 I promised you," Mimi said, reaching into her purse and withdrawing a $10 bill. "Can you start right away?"

"Oh, sure," said the little girl, pocketing the $10 and skipping towards the door with the energy only eleven-year-olds seemed to have. "I'll knock if I find something, or if I've got a question. Thank you, Mrs. Aaron," she said, looking over her shoulder as she went out.

Mimi gave Jonathan an amused glance as Daniella made her way back across the hall to start the search for Rufus.

Chapter thirty-six

"Hello, is this, ah—" he paused and seemed to be riffling through some papers, "Mrs. Aaron?"

"Yes," she said, capturing his voice on the portable phone held between her shoulder and her ear. She had been arranging flowers in the living room, ruminating on her problems, and the telephone had startled her. She had spilled some water. Now she was flustered. She needed to wipe it off before it marked the birds-eye-maple tabletop.

"This is Richard B. Cohen. I'm a veterinarian in Port Chester. I always use my middle initial, you see. There are so many Cohens. There's even another Richard Cohen practicing here."

Mimi's hand went up to grip the phone. Her other hand rose to the pearls at her throat. It had been over a week since they had seen Daniella. She had begun to believe Jonathan had been right. It had been a crazy idea. Now she felt a surge of excitement.

"What can I do for you, Dr. Cohen?" Don't get too

excited. It could be nothing.

"I got your e-mail concerning a lost pug. You know, anytime we get a dog in for treatment, we scan the dog for an owner's chip. Pugs are pretty rare up here, and this one was a beauty. Championship quality, I'd say." He spoke quickly, the words showering over her. "Great bearing. They've been a favorite of mine for years."

"I'm sorry, Dr. Cohen," Mimi said, interrupting, "but can I ask why you're calling?" She suddenly remembered the water spill and went into the kitchen for a dry cloth.

"Oh, of course. Sorry. I love dogs. I got carried away. It's why I became a vet in the first place. And I'm a very good vet."

"I'm sure you are," said Mimi, interrupting the latest digression, "but do you have Rufus?" She wiped at the water spill.

"Sorry. No."

Mimi felt an intense stab of disappointment. "Oh."

But the vet continued. "Well, as I said, we scan every dog."

"What do you mean?" She walked back into the kitchen and dropped the wet dishcloth into the sink.

"I can see you're not a long-time dog owner, Mrs. Aaron. Many owners, particularly of valuable dogs, have a tiny microchip implanted in their dogs. A kind of high-tech collar. It doesn't hurt them. I do it all the time."

"Yes, yes. Please, Dr. Cohen." She felt desperate.

"As I mentioned, I think, I had a pug in yesterday. I had just read your description and I thought it might be your dog. It had the same coloration, and the markings you mentioned seemed similar. Hard to tell without a photo. Often hard to tell even then. Do you have a photo?"

"No, unfortunately." Mimi was giving serious consideration to groveling, something she never had considered before.

"The woman who brought in the dog didn't look like him."

"I beg your pardon."

Cohen chuckled. "I meant not in the class to have a beautiful pug like that. Obviously a purebred. The pug, I mean. But she looked like a retired librarian." Dr. Cohen apparently thought that librarians shouldn't have pure-bred pugs.

"Totally different class," he continued. "And she was very concerned about my fees. No, no. Not in the same class at all."

What a frustrating man. "But didn't you say there was an owner's microchip?"

"No. No. I don't think I said that." He paused. "No, I couldn't have. There was no owner's microchip."

"Please, Dr. Cohen, why did you mention a microchip collar?" Mimi was pleading.

"Oh, there was a microchip, you know."

"No. I didn't know," said Mimi in a resigned voice.

"Of course you didn't." Cohen paused again. "I can see that. But there was. Not an owner's chip. It was a breeder's chip. Lewis Farms. One of the best breeders of pugs in the country. In Virginia. I thought it might be helpful. I called them. They said they'd follow up."

Mimi grabbed a pencil and pad out of the table drawer. "Can you spell Lewis Farms for me? And their telephone number?" She scribbled the information, struggling to keep up. Then she repeated it back to be sure.

"Thank you so much, Dr. Cohen. This is very helpful. And thank you for taking the time to call." She took his telephone number.

"Oh, it's nothing," he said. "You see, I love dogs."

"Thank you," Mimi said again hurriedly and quickly put down the phone to cut off another effusive outburst. Mimi dialed Jonathan.

"I just got a call from a vet in Port Chester. He may have treated Rufus."

"Terrific. Hold on for a minute, Mimi. I just got out of the shower. Let me dry my hair and slip into a robe." The line was silent for a few minutes except for shuffling noises in the background.

"Okay," Jonathan said. "Tell me about it. Do you really think this vet found Rufus?"

She was clearly excited as she described the conversation in somewhat abbreviated terms. They didn't have all day.

"Where's Port Chester?"

"I don't know exactly. A few hours from here, I think."

"Did Rufus come from Lewis Farms?" Jonathan asked. He didn't know breeders implanted chips in their dogs. It made sense.

"I have no idea. I guess Simon would know. Simon gave me some papers, but I gave them to Arthur."

"I'll call Simon and ask him as soon as I get dressed. Give me the information." He made a note. "Don't get too excited. I just hope this is a real lead. I have to tell you, I thought the whole thing was a waste of time."

"Get back to me as soon as you can. I have a good feeling about this. I think it really could be Rufus."

Chapter thirty-seven

"Simon, Jonathan." He was fully dressed now. He wasn't a fan of speaking to Simon Aaron in his underwear. He reached Simon on the private line in his office.

"Hi. What's up?" His tone was flat.

"We may have found Rufus."

"That's just grand," Simon responded in a disinterested voice. "Who's Rufus?"

"The pug you gave to Mimi."

"I gave Mimi a pug?"

"Yeah, you did, Simon. About four months or so ago. She didn't want a dog."

"Oh yeah, I remember now. Cute dog. So?"

"Look, Simon, this is important. It may be essential to solving Mimi's problem."

"So what do you want from me?"

"Did you get a call from Lewis Farms?"

"Who're they?"

"The breeders who sold you Rufus. Don't you remember?"

"Are you kidding? Lauren handles those things." Jonathan pictured china blue eyes, with long legs and short gray hair. He thought Lauren Lucier, Simon's Director of Administration, was probably his most valued employee. Maybe even something more, if he believed some of the rumors he had heard. She ran Simon's life and got options in every deal he did. He had made her rich.

"I wouldn't even know if they called. I didn't speak to them. How do you spell Lewis?" A scratching sound. "Okay, wait a minute." He put the line on hold. He came back on a moment later. "They called and asked for me. We haven't called back yet. Lauren says that's the place we bought the dog."

Bingo. "Mimi and I are going up to Port Chester and see if we can track down Rufus."

"Good luck. Do you think it'll help?" There was a concern there just below the surface. Very unlike Simon Aaron.

"I don't know, but at least it's a loose end that we can tie up. I sure hope so. We don't have anything else to go on."

His next call was to Mimi. There was a hint of excitement in his voice. "Mimi. Simon did purchase Rufus from Lewis Farms. We may have hit the jackpot. Can you call that vet and get the name and address of the lady who brought Rufus in? We need to call her."

"No."

"No?" Would this woman ever stop blindsiding him? "Why, for God's sake?"

"Jonathan, you didn't talk to Dr. Cohen. Once was enough for me. You call him. Please."

"Sure. Give me his number."

* * *

"Dr. Cohen?"

"Yes."

"I'm Jonathan Franklin, a friend of Mimi Aaron's. You called her about a pug that was lost."

"Oh, yes. I love dogs. And I know how it feels to lose one. So I try to help. I consider it part of my job. Veterinary medicine is also one of the healing professions, in my view." The words tumbled out.

"Of course." Jonathan was starting to see the problem and acted to head it off. "Dr. Cohen, I only called to get the name, address and telephone number of the woman who brought in the dog. Can you give that to me?" He ran his hand through his thinning brown hair. It felt thinner than usual.

"Yes, I can. I need to go to my office." The phone went dead for a second. "Let me see now." He started mumbling to himself, and Jonathan could hear papers shuffling in the background. "Ah, here it is. Ms. Sandra Noering. That's N-O-E-R-I-N-G. Do you think that's Scandinavian? She didn't have blond hair."

"I have no idea, Dr. Cohen. Could I have Ms. Noering's address?"

"Well, of course, I don't really know."

"Her address?"

"No. No. I have that right here. I mean her hair color. She had gray hair."

"Excuse me, Dr. Cohen, but could I please have the address and phone number?

"Oh, yes. Of course. It's 63 Vickers St. 614-3173." He repeated the number again slowly. "I'm so glad I could give you that. It makes me feel good. I hope you find your dog. I love dogs, you know."

"Well, thank you, Dr. Cohen," Jonathan said, hanging up fast.

* * *

"Okay, Mimi," Jonathan said, having connected with her, "I've got it. I've arranged for a car and driver. I'll swing by in half an hour and pick you up. Dress warmly. It's really cold out by the ocean." The weather had turned rotten again.

The drive took just over an hour. It was only 25 miles from the city, but the traffic was awful. A crash on I-95, the radio said. Ice on the roads was wreaking havoc. Jonathan felt grateful they were dealing with a lazy kidnapper. He could have driven out a lot further to get rid of the dog.

With a map of Port Chester on his lap, directing the driver right, then left, then right again, they finally found the address. Sandra Noering's small, prim house was on a little side street. It was well kept, but plain, with a tiny garden covered in snow. It looked like the house of a retired librarian. Jonathan knocked and a small woman weighing perhaps 90 pounds, well into her 80s, opened the door a crack. The smell of baking chocolate-chip cookies wafted towards him.

"Ms. Noering."

"Mrs. Please. I don't like all that new-fangled stuff. Can I help you?"

Jonathan started again. "I'm Jonathan Franklin. This is Mimi Aaron." He turned towards Mimi with his hand open, then turned back. "I called. We wanted to see you about your pug."

He pulled up the collar of his overcoat and took off a glove to button the top button. He slipped his hand back into the glove. It was really cold.

"Mrs. Aaron lost a pug, and it's important that she find him." He paused a beat for effect. "It could be a matter of life and death. There's a reward for getting him back. Can you tell us how you got your pug?"

The door was still on the chain. During his speech Mrs. Noering had stood placidly with a smile on her face and wiping her hands on her apron. She looked like a Norman Rockwell painting of everyone's grandmother.

"Won't you come in and have tea? You look cold. I don't often get visitors." Jonathan wasn't sure she'd heard a word he said. The door closed and they heard the chain slide off.

As they entered the house a brown pug came skidding and slipping, tip-tapping to a sliding stop on the hardwood floor. His tail was wagging furiously, and he ran directly up to Mimi.

"Oh, Rufus dear," she said, leaning down to scratch him behind the ears, receiving an enthusiastic licking in return. The pug rolled over onto his back.

She turned her head to Jonathan. "I'm sure this is Rufus. I would know him anywhere." She leaned down to scratch his belly.

Jonathan stooped to pet the dog but withdrew his hand quickly when Rufus emitted a low growl. "I guess I'm not too good with dogs."

"Oh, Mrs. Noering," Mimi said, ignoring him, "thank you so much for taking such good care of Rufus. Can you tell us how you found him?" Mimi looked up.

Mrs. Noering was gone. They caught up with her in her little kitchen, setting the table with fresh-baked cookies and cakes for tea.

"The water will be ready in just a moment. Won't you sit down?" She began pointing out different kinds of sweets. "It's so good to have people in the house. I love to bake. Now what did you want?" she asked, a little vacantly.

Mimi's eyes found Mrs. Noering's unfocused gaze. "How did you find the pug?" Mimi asked gently, smiling at her.

"Oh, I volunteer at the animal shelter. It gets me out of the house. I need that. I was there when he was brought in."

"Mrs. Noering, do you know *who* brought him in?" Jonathan asked quickly.

"Oh, no one. He was brought in by our Animal Control people." Dead end.

She went to the stove and returned with a kettle of boiling water that she poured into the teapot. The smell of brewing tea mixed with the appealing smell of fresh-baked cookies. She let the tea steep for a moment or two and then busied herself pouring for each of them.

"You mentioned you got the dog from the shelter," Jonathan prompted, lifting his cup. He blew on it and took a sip. He remembered why he didn't like tea.

"I loved him at first sight," she said. She smiled at the memory. "Who could resist such a scamp? I brought him home. I named him Dewey, after the decimal system."

Damned if she isn't a librarian.

"He's been a delight. And a good companion. Sometimes I get lonely. It's hard to get out during the winter." She reached for the plate of cookies and cakes and offered them to Mimi. "Won't you have one? I bake them myself."

"Thank you," Mimi said, taking a warm chocolate chip cookie and biting into it. She held up the cookie. "This is delicious."

"I like to bake. I'm glad you like it."

"And I'm glad Rufus has been such a good companion to you," Mimi said.

"He has. But it's a lot of work to take care of him." The old lady glanced down at the dog, who was enthusiastically jumping up and down against Mimi's leg. "He's so energetic. I'm not sure I can manage it at my age." Her eyes reflected a sadness Jonathan thought he grasped.

"When did you find him?" he asked, trying to draw her gently away from her thoughts.

"I remember very well." She perked up, clearly proud of herself. "It was the last day of September. My birthday. I was seeing my son for dinner. He drove all the way up from New York. He's such a good boy. And after that they had me down for dinner just two weeks later."

"Mrs. Noering, would you consider accepting a reward and giving up Rufus?" Mimi asked quietly. "He's very important to us."

"Well—"

"He'll have a good home. We'd be happy to also get you another pug if you want. We're thinking of a $500 reward." It would be a lot of money to a retired librarian. More than Jonathan had contemplated.

"Could I get just a plain dog instead?" She seemed relieved. "I love Dewey—uh, Rufus, but he's really too expensive for me to keep. The veterinarian charges so much. I'm on a fixed income, you know. I had no idea."

"Of course you can. And we'll make the reward $1000. I can tell Rufus has been very happy with you."

Rufus cuddled up against Mimi during the entire ride back. He only lifted his head occasionally to growl at Jonathan, who had moved as far to his side of the car as humanly possible. He was pressed sideways against the back door.

"Mimi, explain to me why we have this dog in the car with us. You told me you didn't want a dog."

"I know. But I couldn't let Rufus stay with strangers. Even a nice old lady like Mrs. Noering. I want him to be with people I care about. He's just so lovable." She looked down at the pug fondly and stroked his head, scratching behind his ear. She turned her quiet eyes towards Jonathan. Rufus growled at him.

"Jonathan, would you mind keeping Rufus for a few days? I really can't keep him right now. My apartment is being cleaned."

Oh, swell! Jonathan thought. The dog hates me. "Look, I might take him for tonight." He spoke reluctantly. "But I'll have to ask Nicole when she gets home tomorrow," he added quickly. "It's her apartment."

He didn't know exactly how, but he was sure this was going to screw things up with Nicole even more. It wasn't just that Nicole had never had a dog. She might be allergic for all he knew. But Christ, even if she likes Rufus, what if she wonders why he doesn't like me? It wasn't a happy thought.

That's all I need now, he didn't say.

Chapter thirty-eight

"Jonathan, it's Mimi." She sounded agitated. It was the day after they had brought Rufus home. Morning sunlight streamed into Nicole's living room through the big windows. Rufus was oblivious. The pug was lying on the couch, snoring, his chin resting on his outstretched paws. "Can you come over to the apartment? I just got some papers from the lawyers, and there's a letter here that's bothering me. Actually, it's bothering me quite a lot."

"Not another letter from Myacura Ishii."

"No. This is different. It's about the estate."

"Is it urgent? Can we make it a little later in the afternoon?" he asked. "I'm right in the middle of something now."

What he was right in the middle of was thinking about how to deal with Nicole, and he wasn't in the mood to be distracted. About a child? About Myacura Ishii? It was hot in the apartment. Had the maid turned up the heat?

"Maybe around three?" he said. "I need to leave in time to get out to JFK by seven to pick up Nicole."

It occurred to Mimi that something was bothering him. He didn't sound as upbeat as usual. She let it pass. "Fine. I'll see you then."

It had been a week since Nicole left. A bad week indeed. His feelings of guilt over Myacura Ishii, along with moments of anxiety when he thought of her brandishing a broken bottle, were eating at him. And his concerns about having a child with Nicole were pressing. When he thought about having a baby, he felt like he couldn't breathe. He paced back and forth in the living room, rubbing his antique silver snuffbox.

It was nearly three.

"I love your dog." "Thanks." "Great dog." "Thank you."

He and Rufus made their way to Mimi's apartment. The cold weather seemed to speed up the city. People didn't want to be out on the streets. Nicole's return was weighing on him. Their telephone calls all week had been reserved, as if they were each holding something back. Jonathan was anxious.

"You brought Rufus." Mimi knelt to scratch the pug behind the ear. "Hello, Rufus dear." He rolled over on his back to get his tummy scratched while his tail thumped madly on the marble floor in the foyer. She looked up at Jonathan. "I'm glad to see you two are getting along."

"We're not. He wouldn't let me come without him. I think he knew I was coming to see you. I'll have to drop him back at the apartment before I go out to pick up Nicole. So maybe we'd better get going."

"Well, thank you for coming," Mimi said. She went over to a small French regency desk and opened a drawer. She took out a letter. "This has really been bothering me. I think Arthur's estate may be in serious trouble." She motioned for them to take a seat. Rufus hopped into her lap. He gazed up at her with his liquid brown eyes. She patted him on the head. "Not now, dear." She smiled down at him before turning to look at Jonathan.

They were surrounded by colorful flowers that were in stark counterpoint to the weather outside the windows. It had turned nasty again since morning. It occurred to him that Mimi must spend a fortune on fresh flowers. Where did New York florists get them in the dead of winter?

She held out a letter. It was addressed to Arthur DeRuk. It was handwritten on beautifully laid paper. The name "Walter Demian" was engraved at the top.

"Who is this guy?" Jonathan asked.

"I've never heard his name before." She shifted to a more comfortable position. Rufus grumbled. She put her manicured finger to her lips and shushed him.

Jonathan settled back to read the letter.

Dear Mr. DeRuk,

I'm upset that you have not had the courtesy to respond to the last letter I sent you over three months ago. Apart from just simple manners towards a collector and an owner of one of your pieces, I would have thought you would show some interest in having your sculpture donated to an important museum. The Tulsa Art Museum has expressed interest in my proposed donation. I always understood that it was important to an artist's reputation and the value of his work

to be represented in the collections of major museums. Per-
haps it is not to yours. However, I would appreciate a reply.

Jonathan adjusted his glasses and continued reading.
So far he didn't get it.

> *I need to know which appraisers you would recommend*
> *to properly value your work. The museum believes the choice*
> *of an appropriate appraiser is vital. They are the ones who*
> *suggested originally that I write to you.*
>
> *As you are no doubt aware, the Internal Revenue Ser-*
> *vice requires an independent appraisal for a donation of this*
> *kind. I own the Artist's Proof of your sculpture entitled the*
> *"Blue Worm."*
>
> *As the end of the year is rapidly approaching I would*
> *appreciate a prompt response. I must complete this gift by*
> *year-end for tax purposes.*
>
> > *Sincerely,*
> > *Walter Demian*

Jonathan looked up. "I don't see the concern, Mimi.
Nothing here seems unusual, except that Arthur DeRuk
was a schmuck and this guy is a little pissed off that he
didn't get an answer to his last letter. I'd be pissed off
too."

"It isn't that, Jonathan. It's what he said about the
sculpture." She fingered the pearls at her neck. "An
'artist's proof' is a copy of a multiple in addition to the
numbered pieces. It's produced as a kind of prototype.
Arthur never created any artist's proofs. He always said
he didn't have to, because his vision was so perfect. It was
one of his eccentricities. I heard him discuss it with
Warren Hovington several times. He was adamant about
it. That's why I remember."

"Uh-oh. So you think this piece is a forgery?"

"Yes. And it scares me. On top of everything else, how do we deal with a forger? It must be quite difficult and expensive to forge a sculpture. It would take a lot of time and very special equipment. If a person does one, it seems to me he's likely to do others. I'm concerned that the value of Arthur's art could be destroyed. Even Warren Hovington was speechless when I told him. He was quite upset."

"I see why you're concerned."

Suddenly a lot of wheels were turning in Jonathan's head. He just couldn't seem to shift them into gear.

Chapter thirty-nine

Nicole had been buttoned up in the American Airlines Boeing 777 for over four hours, and she was getting restless. Pacing the aisle in first class was too short a walk, and she had taken to walking up and down the entire length of the plane. No easy task with the constantly moving service carts. Other passengers were starting to stare. It wasn't like her to be this restless. She made this flight so often. But she was brooding.

Do I really want the responsibility of a child? She rubbed her flat stomach with a manicured hand. I don't know. Would I be a good mother? Do I even like children? No response. Only mental hand wringing. I love my job. I am good at it. Could I still have my career? Would I want to? Why is it so complicated? Her mind seemed to be running away. Why weren't there any answers? A movie flickered on a dozen screens in the main cabin in response to her questions.

She didn't think it was so complicated for other

women. The choice to have a child was the easiest thing in the world. And why did she have to blurt it out to Jonathan like that?

I think I scared him to death. I have never seen him so pale. The thought made her laugh. Serves him right. She started doing knee lifts in the back of the plane.

But maybe it is not so funny. He has sounded so strange on the telephone for the last few days. As if he were closed up. She jumped when the flight attendant spoke.

"Sorry, miss. I need to get past you with the cart." The cart rumbled past as she pressed herself into the bulkhead. "Great. Thanks."

What should she do with him now? She loved the guy. She didn't want him going off the deep end.

Blurting that out really had not been smart. Not for a woman who ran a company of 2000 employees with operations all over the world. One would have thought I would have learned something. She started back down the aisle to first class.

Back in her seat, her mind was anything but settled. She flipped through the airline magazine again. Her eyes didn't focus. She started to get up again when the intercom clicked on.

"Please take your seats and fasten your seat belts. We're expecting some mild turbulence. Nothing to worry about. I'll let you know when it's safe to move around again. Thanks."

With a sigh, she sank back into her leather seat.

Finally, finally, the plane landed. She was one of the first passengers off and through customs. There was Jonathan, waiting outside the doors, waving. She ran up to him and threw her arms around his neck. Then she held him away to look at him with warm gray eyes that lit up her face.

"*Cheri*," she said, giving him a long, slow, lingering kiss, "I missed you so much." He could feel her lithe body pressed against him through his clothes. This wasn't what he'd expected. He'd thought she'd be reserved. Even mad at him.

"*Cheri*." It came out all in a rush. "I do not know what possessed me. Will you forgive me?"

"For what?"

"Wanting a child."

"Wanting a child? Of course I forgive you. I understand." People flowed around them, a few looking back over their shoulders, attracted by their intensity. "You just took me by surprise, darling," he said with an inaudible sigh of relief.

"This is something about which we both must be certain. I am not sure either that I want a child."

Thank God she had doubts too. The same kind of doubts he had. "I love you," he said. I'm so glad you're back." He hugged her again. "The car's waiting outside. Let's get your baggage. Button up your coat. It's cold."

They were holding hands and happily chatting as the elevator opened on the floor of Nicole's apartment. Then he remembered. Damn. He put his hand on her arm and pulled her to a stop as she was searching in her purse for the key.

"Uh, darling."

"Yes?" She looked up at him quizzically.

"Mimi asked—I told her I'd ask you—it's a dog." Not his most articulate self.

"What is a dog?"

"Well, you see, we went to Port Chester and found this pug and Mimi couldn't keep him and she asked—"

"We have a pug?" She gave a little shriek and clapped her hands. "I love pugs! What is his name?"

"Rufus."

"That is adorable."

"Well, this one can be pretty obnoxious. All he ever does is growl at me. We don't have to keep him for long."

"Is he here?"

"Yes."

"Oh, I cannot wait. What a wonderful surprise."

She opened the door to find Rufus sitting in the foyer, looking up at her with deep brown eyes, his tongue lolling out, panting and wagging as he rose.

"He is beautiful," she said scooping him up in her arms and twirling around. Rufus was licking her wherever he could reach.

"Oh, *cheri*, can we keep him?"

Jonathan felt a little twinge of jealousy but also a surge of relief. He nodded.

"Thank you! Oh, thank you! He is wonderful."

Jonathan watched as she drew the pug in close to her breast. She was treating Rufus like a child. Was that bad or good?

It was early the next morning when Jonathan rolled quietly out of bed. Rufus lay snoring softly on the floor on Nicole's side. She was still asleep. As he made his way to the door of the bathroom, he looked back. In the dim dancing light her face was relaxed and innocent, framed by her short dark hair. He felt a rush of warmth wash over him.

"Whatever more could I ask for?" he said, half in wonder, as a cold shadow of guilt passed through him.

Chapter forty

"What is art?"

It popped out just like that. He was almost as surprised as Nicole was. They were sitting in their bathrobes at the breakfast table the morning after her return. The question made Nicole laugh. Her smile reached all the way to her gray eyes. Rufus raised his head and looked at her. When he realized he wasn't going to get petted or fed, he returned to dozing under the table.

"Could you not ask me a broader question?" she said as she tried her coffee.

"No, seriously. I was with Warren Hovington, and beyond the fact that the man is a pretentious ass, he was saying things that undermined my whole idea of what art is. Apparently Arthur DeRuk couldn't even draw well. He 'conceptualized,' to quote Hovington."

"It is an important question." She became pensive. "And of course there is no answer."

"Swell. Can you be more specific?"

"I will try." She put down her cup. "To start, I try to approach art on three levels. First, emotionally. Does it reach me on a visceral level? Then, intellectually. What is the artist trying to say through his creation? Finally, technically. How well is the piece executed?"

"That's easy enough. But what does it mean?"

"Ah, there you have the difficulty, *cheri*. Sometimes this approach does not apply. A good deal of contemporary art is highly intellectual. The idea predominates over all else. And much of contemporary art does not recognize beauty as being of importance."

"I just don't get it." He let loose his growing frustration. "If the idea predominates, how can you judge anything?"

"One question you must ask yourself is whether the idea is important, and whether the work is derivative."

"Okay, I give up."

She gave him a small smile. "*Cheri*, you are asking me to explain all of modern art to you over breakfast. It is difficult. A work is derivative if it too closely relates to a previous work or idea. Of course, influence is universal and to be admired." She laughed. Rufus raised his head and licked her bare foot. She leaned down and scratched him behind the ear. His tail beat a tattoo on the wooden floor.

"Right," he said. She straightened and glanced across at him. "So I have to know enough to make sure a work —or, God forbid, an idea—is not too closely related to someone else's work, although a little alike, but not too much, is admirable? Have I got that straight?"

When he said it that way, it made the whole thing sound ridiculous. She shrugged and went on a little desperately. He caught a subtle whiff of French perfume as she moved.

"You must develop what we call an eye for this. It is very much a matter of judgement and taste. Even experts disagree. That is why it is so difficult. But if a work is original, that does not mean it is significant. Whether the art is important or lasting is yet another question. Many artists fade and some are resurrected or even discovered after their deaths."

"But it's nonsense to talk about conceptualizing a piece in an environment to bring out its inner meaning," he said.

"Well, if you are speaking of Arthur DeRuk, he certainly was controversial. Deliberately so, I think. He loved the publicity and it served him well." Jonathan sipped at his coffee as he watched her. He loved the way her gray eyes sparked when she talked about art. "It helped his work sell. He was the bad boy of New York art circles. But he was not the first, of course. You could say the same for many that came before him. I always considered his work ordinary, but others found it deep and important. To them it represented ideas in almost their purest form."

Clouds were rolling in and one momentarily blocked the sun, casting a shadow on the table. "But how do you distinguish an artist from a publicity-loving fraud?"

Nicole shrugged again. "Perhaps just by how serious an artist he is. Or how serious he was, in Arthur DeRuk's case. Must one be technically capable to be an artist?" Her hand made a graceful arc. "We will be certain in a hundred years."

It was an explanation that he found neither comforting nor illuminating. He gave up.

"What do you know about Hovington?"

"Personally, I do not like him," she said. "I find him too stiff."

He caught a glimpse of her bare breast as she turned to refill her coffee cup. He reached over and slipped his hand inside her robe. She jumped and slapped at his hand with a playful yip. "Not until after your lesson. You started this."

A low growl rumbled from under the table.

"Now, where was I?" she said. "Oh, yes, someone was 'stiff.'" Her playful eyes found his. He reached under the table to adjust his robe where it had poked open, wondering just where Rufus was.

"As to Warren Hovington, I find him too full of himself. He has been a dealer in contemporary art for many years here in New York. His reputation is somewhat clouded. My dealings with him have been satisfactory, but financially we at Witten's are cautious of him."

The light in the apartment was shifting again, letting shadows play along the breakfast room. It was a comfortable room with its view over Central Park. It felt like being in Paris. Maybe that's why Nicole liked it. Why she moved back in after her father's death. They sat in silence for a bit, enjoying each other's presence.

"Mimi Aaron told me a strange thing," he said, breaking the silence. It occurred to him there was something he should ask Nicole. "There were four DeRuk pieces that sold in the last contemporary art auction at Witten's. They brought record prices. You know Mimi is the executor of DeRuk's estate," he added, making a quick circle-back.

"Yes. You mentioned it."

"When she tried to get the money from Hovington for the pictures, he said he had to refund the money to three buyers. Some irregularities. He produced his canceled checks. He paid the buyers. And he had the art pieces back. She can't make heads or tails of it."

Nicole smiled knowingly. "I can perhaps. I would not be surprised if those buyers were people who were acting for Warren Hovington. He may have been seeking to increase the price on Arthur DeRuk's work. If DeRuk's work is worth more, he makes more money from the sale of the art. Both on those pictures he owns, and those he will sell for the estate. It is not unknown among art dealers, you know. It is not ethical, but it is also not illegal."

Another dead-end.

Chapter forty-one

They were having a lazy kind of day. Breakfast had been cut short for play, and now they had showered and dressed. It was almost lunchtime. Nicole and Jonathan had decided to stay in. The snow had started again and was falling in soft, drifting flakes.

"It really looks dark out there," he said. "I'm glad to be inside."

"With you, *cheri*." She snuggled in closer and laid her head on his shoulder.

A fire played yellow and red in the fireplace, casting its warmth across the living room. They cuddled on the big couch. Rufus lay on his back under Nicole's feet, being idly petted with her slippered toes, his tongue lolling to one side. He had a distant, happy look in his brown eyes. His tail beat the rug.

"I'm glad your trip was successful," Jonathan said after a while. "It sounds like the spring auction schedule is shaping up. You've done a great job."

"Were you good while I was away?" she asked, catching his eyes with a smile. Her hand lay on his chest.

Jonathan had a sharp pang of guilt and struggled to maintain a lawyerly face. He shifted in his seat.

"Well, it was interesting," he said. He didn't want to lie, but he certainly didn't want to tell her the truth. He felt bad enough as it was. And honesty wasn't always the best policy in his experience.

"Simon really set me up with that Zager partnership interest," he said, launching into a new subject. "It's a great winery but it's a very tough business." She nodded, only half listening. "There could be some large capital calls. Day Zager and his wife Barbara are terrific people. You have to meet them. Zager's a great storyteller."

Jonathan unwound himself and got up to make a note. "Sorry, darling," he said. He sat down again and put his arm around her. He drew her in closer. "Something just clicked. I need to discuss it with Mimi tomorrow. I'm still worried about her."

"Have you found anything?"

Jonathan shook his head. "I wish. Anyway, when we get out to California we'll pay the Zagers a visit."

"Ummm. Sunshine, good wine and interesting people. I would look forward to that. But I do love the snow." She looked out the window at the gray sky with its drifting white flakes. It created a sense of silence broken only by the crackling of the fire. "When I can sit here with you."

"Me too." He hugged her. "But you'll like the Zagers. Day Zager used to be a doctor. But he looks happier now than most doctors do. You'll be interested in how the wine business is run. It's different than the auction business but I'll bet the customers are a lot alike. It's always seemed to me that the wine and food circles overlap a lot with the art people. You may even find it useful."

Rufus had shifted from being petted to licking Nicole's ankle. "Silly dog," she said, leaning over, stroking his head. She turned back towards Jonathan, who was watching this display with bemusement. "How did you find this sweet puppy?"

He pulled her to him. "There was nothing else to do. We were completely stumped." He shrugged a shoulder and kissed the top of her head. "It was Mimi's idea. I thought it was dumb. But she got this eleven-year-old little computer genius to put out a statewide search on the Internet. You should have seen this kid." He fiddled with his glasses to get them to sit straight. "And damn if a vet didn't call. So we went to Port Chester and found Rufus with this nice old lady."

She looked down at Rufus, who had rolled over on his back again and was staring up at her, his paws folded in. "He looks like he was wonderfully cared for. How long did she have him?" She rubbed his belly with her toe.

"Oh, about two months. She got him from the animal shelter on September 30th. Can you believe she remembered the date?" Then it hit him. The thought drew him upright in the chair. "Damn! How could I have been so dumb!" He struggled to his feet. "Sorry, darling I just realized something. I've got to call Mimi right away."

"Mimi, it's Jonathan." There was excitement in his voice. Things were finally starting to fall into place. "Do you remember the date that Mrs. Noering picked up Rufus? Yeah, that's the same one I recall. You told me that Rufus was kidnapped about four weeks before DeRuk died." He tapped his fingers on the tabletop.

"Okay, a little over a month. Was the ransom call made right away? A day or two later. That would make it October 1 or 2." He shifted the phone to his other hand and grabbed a pencil to make a note of her response. "You see it now, don't you? Yeah, so do I," he said. "It's as plain as the nose on my face. I was really dense. The kidnapper let Rufus loose before he called DeRuk. There never was any intention of returning him. Right. There must have been some other reason. Yes. You know, I think so too."

Jonathan was silent for a while as Mimi talked. "I couldn't agree with you more. We need to sit down and see where we go with this. It puts it all in a new light, doesn't it? And I think I may also have found another piece of the puzzle."

He reached for his topcoat. Hot damn.

Chapter forty-two

The wind had picked up, blowing the snow. It was the coldest day yet. His questions had driven him out of his home without lunch to seek out Mimi Aaron. He had buttoned his topcoat askew in his haste.

"Taxi." He held up his hand. The Statue of Liberty pose. "Taxi." Damn, where were the empty cabs? He felt like his ears were going to fall off. "Taxi!" A cab pulled over. "Fifth Avenue and Seventy-First," he said, climbing into the warmth.

"Mimi, the police think there was foul play in Arthur DeRuk's death. And they suspect you because you had motive, means and opportunity." He was being emphatic. Maybe even harsh. Leaning forward towards Mimi, he realized he resented being here. Damn it, he wanted to be home with Nicole. Why was he involved in this anyway? He hardly knew Mimi Aaron. Maybe he was just hungry.

He got this way when he missed his lunch.

Mimi's eyes flashed and she made a dismissing motion with her hand. "You've said that before." Her voice had an edge to it. She got up and started fiddling with some flowers.

Jonathan forged ahead. "Look, I need to go through this. I'm sorry if it upsets you, but we have to understand where we are. From Lieutenant Wayne's point of view, you're the jilted jealous lover who profits from DeRuk's death. You have no alibi for the time of his death. In fact, you were behaving suspiciously. You used your key to get in and probably found him unconscious. You found where he kept his stash, if you didn't know beforehand, and injected him with another hit of heroin that happened to have even more wallop. It didn't matter. A regular hit would have done the job."

"Jonathan, this is nonsense. Why are you going on like this? Are you trying to frighten me?"

"No." He deflated into his seat. "I'm sorry. Do you have anything to eat? I rushed over without lunch."

They were in the kitchen. It was twenty minutes and a grilled cheese sandwich later. He wiped milk off his mouth with a flowered cloth napkin.

"Thanks, I get a little testy on an empty stomach."

"I'll say."

"But look, let me go on a little. I may be on to something, and it helps me think to lay it out."

She picked up his plate and glass and walked to the sink. "It's Maria's day off," she said.

He spoke with her back to him. He raised his voice over the running water. "The police think you called them with a cock-and-bull story because you knew they'd look for a syringe, and if you wiped it clean they'd know something was wrong. It would be a pretty smart move, really. You and I know that's not what happened. But we have to do something to help them focus on someone else. Anyone else. As it is, I'm sure they haven't been more aggressive because everything they have so far is circumstantial."

She looked back at Jonathan over her shoulder. She was scrubbing the plate with a sponge. He walked over to the sink to join her. "Here, let me dry." He took the plate and wiped it. She passed him the wet glass.

"It sounds awful when you say it," she said. "About what the police think, I mean. What can we do? You talked about Rufus when you called. But I still don't see how he fits in."

"Well, it's complicated, and if I'm right it's very subtle. There were lots of people with an obvious motive. Quinn, Myacura Ishii. Quinn hated Arthur DeRuk's guts. He caused his bankruptcy and divorce. Ruined his life. DeRuk dumped Ishii. Humiliated her. She despised him. And you as well. Even Hovington could have had a motive. His relationship with DeRuk was complicated enough. But everyone has an alibi." He started for the kitchen table and stopped. "Would you mind if we went back into the living room? I like the light."

"What are you getting at, Jonathan?"

"It was the letter DeRuk got from that man that the lawyers sent over to you. The one who wanted to donate the artist's proof to the Tulsa Art Museum. It was something you said. It got me thinking. I just couldn't put it together."

He leaned forward and tapped on the coffee table.

"If you can get me some documents I need to see, I might be able to get some answers. I'll know then if I'm right or just having hallucinations."

"What do you need?" She was eager. It was the first time any light had broken into the darkness of this nightmare.

"DeRuk didn't do his own sculpture. Warren Hovington told me that. He had a foundry do it for him, right?"

"Yes. Cremonti & Sons. They're the leading house for that kind of thing." Her tone was puzzled.

"Can you get me a copy of all their invoices? You have to get it directly from them. I don't want anyone to know we're asking. It might spook someone. Make up some excuse as DeRuk's executor. It shouldn't be hard."

She fixed her gray-green eyes intently on his face. "Jonathan, I have no idea how this is going to help, but I believe I can do that. How should I get them to you?"

"I'll pick them up. Call me." He was anxious. "If I'm right, I'll need to pay a visit to our Lieutenant Wayne."

"Do you want to tell me what you're thinking?"

"It's just too far out. I'm either totally off base or you were right. DeRuk was murdered. And Rufus really was the answer. I just hope I'm not barking up the wrong tree." Jonathan smiled at his pun.

Mimi didn't. She went to the telephone and started dialing.

Chapter forty-three

"Franklin, I knew you were an idiot when I first set eyes on you. That's just plain nuts." Homicide Lieutenant Julian Wayne was leaning back in his chair, eyeing Jonathan over the tops of his scuffed shoes. There was a hole in one sole.

Jonathan had just told him who committed the murder of Arthur DeRuk. Wayne wasn't buying.

"I appreciate your confidence, Lieutenant. But I can lay out all the pieces for you. Prove me wrong. It's your job."

Wayne came forward with a thump. "Don't tell me what my job is, damn it." His fist struck the desk. The ever present half-cup of cold coffee sloshed onto an assortment of papers strewn on the surface and started to soak in. Wayne disregarded it. He was wearing a dark tie over a mismatched plaid shirt. The office was uncomfortably hot. He apparently wasn't taking any chances on another cold.

"There's a crime here anyway," Jonathan persevered. "Grand larceny. We're filing a complaint on behalf of the estate. You're going to have to investigate it. I just thought I should try to help you tie it all together."

"This I gotta hear."

"It all starts with the old bartender's trick, you see."

"Sure, why didn't I think of that?"

"No, really. It was the motive, or at least the reason the murder was committed."

"Before you enlighten me on that, maybe you want to tell me how. You know there's a solid alibi."

"Time shifting."

"Yeah? Are we talking time travel here?"

"No." Jonathan's lips offered a thin smile. Wayne was a good cop. That didn't mean he had to like him. "It's like you program a VCR to record a show you want to see later when you get home."

"So what does a television show have to do with this so-called murder?"

"It doesn't. The murder was time-shifted. A bag of very high-grade heroin was put in Arthur DeRuk's stash. It was bagged to look like all the other bags. It was only a matter of time until he shot himself up and died."

"He was on the wagon." Wayne's fierce brown eyes were fixed on Jonathan. "Been clean for months."

"As Mrs. Aaron told you, Lieutenant, it was the dog that did it. When Rufus was kidnapped, DeRuk broke down and fell hard off the wagon. DeRuk was high-strung. He was always susceptible to stress. You just had to know how to apply the pressure properly. It was easy if you knew DeRuk's character and habits. Access wasn't a problem. Everyone had a key to his apartment. He gave them out like candy."

"Okay, what's the motive? I don't see it."

"That's where the bartender's trick comes in. DeRuk discovered the murderer had his hand in the cookie jar. He got a letter from a collector named Walter Demian before his death. He realized something was wrong."

Inspector Bobby Tritter stuck his head into the office and ducked out quickly when he saw the look on Wayne's face.

"Warren Hovington was stealing from him," Jonathan said. "Hovington was more than his art dealer, he was DeRuk's keeper. He handled everything, including the relationships with DeRuk's suppliers. Once DeRuk conceptualized a piece, Hovington had all the dealings with the foundry that cast them."

"Are you telling me this guy was making forgeries?"

"No, not exactly. Hovington was a lot smarter than that. He would have a series of 8 or 12 cast as DeRuk instructed. That's the way sculpture is done. Hovington would then order an extra piece and have it marked 'Artist's Proof.' It's a common practice. Most sculptors do it. They use it as a test piece, then they sell it later and make a little extra money. No one at the fabricators would have the least suspicion. Only DeRuk never had artist's proofs cast. It was an eccentricity. Mimi Aaron told me about it. He must have confronted Hovington. That wouldn't have been pretty. DeRuk wasn't a nice man. He must have threatened to expose him. Hovington couldn't allow that."

The detective watched him, waiting.

"Hovington knew how DeRuk felt about the pug. He was in and out of DeRuk's apartment all the time. DeRuk loved that puppy like a child. Not that I can understand why. Anyway, when I realized that the kidnapper let the dog go before he made the ransom call, I knew there had to be another reason for the kidnapping. And Hovington also must have realized at some point how much more DeRuk was worth to him dead than alive."

"Exactly how do you know all this?"

Jonathan ignored the question. "Hovington was clever. The value of DeRuk's work would skyrocket. All the pieces his gallery owned would go up in value."

"Why?"

"No more pieces. The law of supply and demand. Hovington also gets paid as art executor. His fees would increase as the value of the art owned by the estate went up. He would control that art. And then there was the catalog raisonne. That's a book describing every authentic piece of DeRuk's art works. That was the really bright part."

"Yeah?"

"I started wondering why Hovington would spend the time to do it. He said he felt an obligation to DeRuk. But it was a lot of work and he wouldn't be paid. There was no money in the estate. He was a guy with financial problems. It just didn't make sense."

Again Wayne waited. There was something predatory about him.

Jonathan kept going. "After we found out about the extra pieces, it all fell into place. Brilliant, really. A catalog raisonne would validate all the pieces Hovington had sold. He was off the hook. But the really clever part was that it set up all the pieces Hovington was going to sell in the future. They would be certified DeRuk sculptures. They wouldn't belong to the estate, and he could sell a couple a year forever. No more financial troubles. I just don't know whether he figured it all out before he killed DeRuk or it occurred to him afterwards."

The detective's eyes never left him. The silence stretched out.

"And it could never come out because the estate would be able to track all its inventory. Nothing would ever be missing. He'd benefit in every way. But with DeRuk alive, Hovington would have been disgraced. It couldn't have been a hard choice for him. And it might have been a perfect crime. Except that Hovington couldn't kill the dog. He was too cute, and Hovington loved animals. He was involved in animal charities."

"Why're you tellin' me this?"

"Two reasons." Jonathan leaned forward, placing both his hands on Wayne's desk. "First, Mimi Aaron shouldn't be living under a cloud. She's my friend. Second, we have some proof but we can't go the next step."

He pulled a sheath of copies out of his leather portfolio and handed them across to Wayne. "Those are copies of the fabricator's invoices," he said, jabbing towards the papers in Wayne's hand. "You can see what they delivered to Hovington. The Artist's Proofs. There." Jonathan pointed at a place on the invoice. He was reading upside down. An old lawyer's trick.

"You can bet these invoices never made their way to DeRuk," Jonathan said. "At least, not like this. But that's just theft. The rest of it's a theory. It all fits together, but we can't do the police work to prove it. You can."

Wayne leaned back in his chair. "Okay. We'll look into it. Maybe you're smarter than you look." He didn't sound convinced.

"If I'm right, Lieutenant, I'll be happy to introduce you to Rufus. He's the one we should both thank."

Maybe he'll bite you, Jonathan thought. And I'll kill two birds with one stone.

Chapter forty-four

She was holding up a glass of '98 Zager Reserve Pinot Noir. The light refracted through the deep ruby color. Her face lit up with a broad smile.

"Here's to you, Jonathan. You're everything that Simon said." Mimi paused dramatically. "Or in Simon's case, didn't say. Thank you."

"Hear! Hear!" added Nicole and Simon. They clinked glasses. The four of them were sitting at a banquette in a corner of La Grenouille. The holiday spirit was upon them all. That included Rufus, who was lying between Nicole and Jonathan on the burgundy cushion, enjoying Nicole's hand stroking his back. It was three days before New Year's. It had been a glorious Christmas. The best Jonathan could ever recall.

The restaurant was empty. He remembered the bustle at Smith & Wollensky. Was the economy suddenly that bad again, or did Simon buy the place out to celebrate in private? He suspected the latter. It was Simon's style.

"While I just hate to admit it, I was somewhat uncomfortable," Mimi said.

I hope that's an understatement, Jonathan thought.

"But I'm glad it's over and the police have arrested Warren Hovington," she said. "I'm much happier now that a reputable dealer has been appointed Arthur's art executor. Nicole, thank you for introducing me to your cousin, Henri DeSant. I feel Arthur's reputation is in good hands."

Nicole put down her fork, her mouth full, and nodded to Mimi. She chewed deliberately and swallowed. Then she turned towards Jonathan. "I was surprised the police arrested Warren Hovington so quickly," she said.

"Well, it wasn't too hard to find the evidence once you knew where to look," Jonathan said. "Hovington had a coke dealer. The police put the arm on him and found out that Hovington had made a purchase of two bags of heroin about three months ago. It was the first and only time." A waiter hovered nearby, and Jonathan paused until Simon shooed him away.

"The police think Hovington precipitated out the sugar used to cut the heroin and combined the bags," he continued when the waiter was gone. "It would be pretty potent stuff. With his key, Hovington had no problem getting in when DeRuk was out and placing the bag in DeRuk's stash. He knew more about DeRuk than DeRuk's own mother did. Then he just scooped up Rufus and bundled him off. Rufus was probably more than happy to go for a ride." Rufus looked up at Jonathan at the sound of his name.

Nicole picked up the pug, who was furiously wagging his tail at the attention, and placed him on the floor so she could slide closer to Jonathan. She kicked off a shoe and started to rub Rufus' soft belly fur with her stockinged toe. Rufus rolled over onto his back in contentment.

Jonathan leaned towards her and whispered in her ear, "You know, I really love you. I never want to lose you."

She leaned into him. "Nor I you. You should remember, *cheri*, what your great ancestor Benjamin Franklin said about potential husbands." She picked up her wineglass and lifted it to him. She gazed meaningfully into his eyes. "A good husband is worth two good wives."

Jonathan preened a little. It was nice to be appreciated. "Dr. Franklin was always wise, dear. But why did he say that?"

"Because scarcity creates value, *cheri*."

She burst out laughing. Jonathan joined her a moment later as he thought it through. Simon and Mimi turned to look at them. There were tears in their eyes, they were laughing so hard.

"Okay," Jonathan whispered in her ear when he caught his breath. "That's it. You better marry me and make me an honest man."

She nodded. There were tears in her deep gray eyes, but now they weren't tears of laughter. They both were quiet for a moment. He kissed her and tasted the red wine on her lips. Then he hugged her against him and closed his eyes. He buried his face in her short dark hair. He loved the way she smelled. She folded her legs under her on the banquette. Beneath the table, Jonathan heard Rufus stir.

After a few moments, Jonathan opened his eyes and looked over at Simon. "You know, Simon, I'm reminded of something," he said, moving away from Nicole. He had unfinished business.

"Oh, about what?" Simon looked up from his coq au

vin. He didn't seem too impressed.

"I've been thinking about writing a book. I've always wanted to, but I never got around to it."

"Does the world need another law book?" Simon asked with bare politeness.

"Not that. A mystery."

"Great. What's it about?" Simon had lifted his wine glass, paying half attention now.

"You know, I've been thinking about the first time you asked me to help you. Back in '98, when Witten's was in trouble and about the problems you had. When I first met Nicole. When her fortune was at stake. I think it would make a great story."

"Are you out of your mind?" Simon said, sitting up straighter, anxiety creeping into his voice. He put down his glass hard enough to make a dribble of red wine stain the white linen tablecloth. "You can't do that. What . . . what about the attorney-client privilege?" he added. He was grasping.

"Nope, doesn't apply. Remember, I told you I wasn't acting as your lawyer."

"But—but. It'll make me look bad."

"Are you kidding?" Jonathan said with a serious face. "I'm going to make you into a great Tonto."

"Tonto!" Simon seemed to deflate. He sunk back into his seat. "Okay, okay. What do you want to forget the whole idea?"

"Well, now—" Jonathan said and deliberately fell into silence.

"Come on."

"You know we just got a two-million-dollar capital call from Day Zager for the new vineyard land."

"Of course I know."

"And you remember how you took advantage of me

when you gave me the interest in Zager to get me to help Mimi."

"Well—" Simon even sounded a little chagrined.

Amazing, Jonathan thought.

"How about another five percent?" Simon offered, perking up.

Back to the old Simon.

"Simon, that's not quite what I had in mind."

Simon managed to sound astonished. "What do you want?"

"I want you to pay my capital calls."

"You mean this one."

"All of them."

Simon looked like he was going to go into a pout until Mimi stepped in.

"Simon," she said, fixing him with a glare. She did it very well, Jonathan noticed.

"Oh, all right," Simon surrendered, still somehow conveying thoughts of his wounded sensitivities in only those few words.

Jonathan's satisfied smile suddenly changed to puzzlement. He felt like there was a wet spot on his pant leg. That wasn't possible.

He glanced down as he felt the warm wet spot spreading and met Rufus' contented gaze. He could swear the damn dog was smiling at him.

—THE END—